Wings
— AND —
Roots

Other books by Susan Terris

No Scarlet Ribbons
Stage Brat
Tucker and the Horse Thief
The Chicken Pox Papers
Two P's in a Pod
The Pencil Families
Whirling Rainbows
Plague of Frogs
The Drowning Boy
On Fire
No Boys Allowed
Amanda, the Panda, and the Redhead
The Backwards Boots
The Upstairs Witch and the Downstairs Witch

WINGS
— AND —
ROOTS

Susan Terris

FARRAR · STRAUS · GIROUX · *New York*

For Yeti

night it was and, as always, i was alone in the dark, aching and empty, but still flying through layers of cool clouds. flying on and on using arms, dragging legs like some ponderous prehistoric bird, for it was hard to fly and i was heavy and filled with pain, but there was no place to stop, no place to rest, and no one's hands reaching up to take hold of me.

YETI

Summer 1955

1

A WASP was exploring the Occupational Therapy room. Jeannie West watched it veer and careen, kissing the shiny white walls until it found its way back out the open window. For a moment, she looked after it longingly, wishing that she had wings to carry her out of Hanover Hospital into the warm, honeysuckle air of San Francisco on a June morning.

Then, pursing her lips, she wrapped a starched yellow apron around herself, tying it firmly at the waist. By pulling the apron strings uncomfortably tight, she hoped to make her fourteen-year-old scarecrow body look more adult, more responsible.

She was, she reminded herself, a special case. She was not a Pink Lady—one of the uniformed corps of women volunteers who roamed the hospital. She was one of a kind. Dr. Martin Storey's young niece, the tall skinny kid who was interested in medicine and was working for the summer in the post-polio ward at Hanover.

The uniqueness of her status was a source of embarrassment. In a hospital blooming with white, green, and pink uniforms, she wore the lone yellow apron, a reject tossed to her by Mary Markham, who ran the Occupational Therapy—or O.T.—department. Jeannie, to make her outfit seem more official, wore a white blouse and skirt beneath it. After two weeks, though, she still felt like a yellow weed that had sprung up in a manicured garden.

When she walked through the halls, crabbed whispers pinched at her. "Young Storey's niece," they said. "Martin's sister's girl." Those whispers often reminded her that her best friend, Lisabeth, was spending an easy summer at camp. Over kind, well-meaning objections from her mother and father, Jeannie had made her choice, so now—like it or not—she would stick to it. She wasn't always right, but she never started anything she didn't intend to finish.

With this thought uppermost in her mind, she pulled herself back into the present. It was Thursday. On Thursdays, when Mary Markham had her day off, Jeannie was a whole department by herself. Turning away from the open window, she piled up a stack of game boxes and a supply of coloring books. It was time to distribute them to the patients.

When she was picking up her wares, something on the bulletin board caught her eye. She paused. It was a piece of three-ring notebook paper filled with a stream of words printed out in stiff lowercase letters and signed by a name written all in capitals—another message from Yeti.

Jeannie turned back. Letters from the mysterious Yeti tugged at her. As she read them, she always wondered who could be writing such things.

Yeti was the talk of the whole ward. One day the messages had simply started appearing. Sometimes they were on bulletin boards, sometimes on the glass partition at the nursing station, sometimes by the elevator, in the bathrooms, or over the scales. If anyone knew who Yeti was, no one admitted it. Though old messages came down and new ones appeared, no one saw any patient or any nurse putting them up.

Gripping the games more tightly against her chest,

Jeannie moved in close enough to bring Yeti's tiny printing into clearer focus.

first i was dead wrapped in shrouds of icy cirrus, then i was a wrinkled baby again, crying in a wet bed, crying to be changed and fed, weeping because my head felt like a thousand beetles were boring into it, weeping as ghoulish doctors stood over my bed saying, as if i had no ears, that i might die like the boy who had been drowning in the bed next to me, who had disappeared behind secret white curtains at two one morning never to reappear. where did they take you, boy, where, oh where? silently i cried, desolate because i wasn't strong enough to slip my thumb in my mouth.

                                                                    YETI

With a shiver, Jeannie wrenched her eyes away from the message and, with as firm a step as she could manage, headed down the long corridor toward the ward. Walking in there was never easy, but stepping in after reading words from Yeti was especially difficult. Yellow walls and Disney murals couldn't camouflage the presence of cold steel. Steel bed frames, wheelchairs, and braces were everywhere. And looming in the back corner—the row of hissing monsters which the doctors called respirators but the patients called iron lungs.

Taking a deep breath, she moved tentatively through the double doorway. At ten, the ward was fairly quiet. Bed baths were in progress. Some patients were upstairs in physical therapy. Jeannie felt shy, anxious about barging in.

As she walked slowly down aisle A, she examined each bed for signs of a welcoming face. Little red-haired Karen was dozing. A boy known as Tooter was sobbing for his

5

mother. Jeannie felt as if the bottoms of her shoes were coated with slow-drying layers of Lepage's glue. She was thinking about Yeti lying in a bed somewhere, hearing doctors say he was going to die. She was so preoccupied with thoughts of Yeti that it took her some time to realize a voice was calling out to her.

"Nurse! Nurse!"

The voice was high-pitched, harsh, demanding. Jeannie didn't turn her head. She hated being addressed in that tone.

"Hey, you! Nurse!"

She stiffened her shoulders, shifted her grasp on the games, but she didn't turn.

"Nurse! Damn it—pick up my pencil!"

That voice was irritating. She wanted to drop her load right on the head of whoever was speaking to her. "I'm not a nurse," she replied, still refusing to look back.

"Well, orderly, Pink Lady, LVN—whatever—pick up my pencil!"

"My arms are full. Can't you pick it up yourself?"

"No," the voice answered with a trace of a self-pitying whine. "I'm a polio."

Jeannie spun around and fixed her eyes on the person— the boy with the nagging, commanding voice. He was lying on his stomach on a gurney with a cotton sheet thrown over his body. He had dark-blond hair that curled softly above pale eyes, which were a little too close together.

"I said, I'm a polio."

Jeannie frowned. "What?"

"I am a polio. I want my pencil. Do you understand English?"

"You're not a *polio*," Jeannie declared, repeating words she'd learned from her uncle. "You are a person

6

who has had paralytic poliomyelitis. And they have moved you down from the acute ward because you're not contagious any more."

The boy gripped the edges of the gurney so hard that his knuckles looked like tiny ice cubes. He seemed to be trying to figure out how he could rise up and strangle her. "Who says I'm not contagious? You? You're not a nurse. You're a kid. Get out of here. I don't want to see you. Get lost!"

Jeannie began backing away from him. She thought he had made an excellent suggestion. She felt it would probably be a long time before she came this far down aisle A again.

Then, suddenly, she stopped. Something about this boy's manner, his anger, struck a chord in her. "Tell me something," she began, being uncharacteristically direct, "are you Yeti?"

"Are you Florence Nightingale's illegitimate daughter?" he said. "What are you doing here, anyway? Don't your parents love you? Do they want you to end up a no-good cripple like me? Go play in Fleishhaker Pool if you want to get polio—that would be more fun than catching it in Hanover Hospital. What *are* you doing here? Are you some kind of wonk?"

Jeannie leaned back against an empty bed. The boy's barrage of questions swirled around in her head like a tornado, and all she could remember clearly was the last one he had asked. "What's a wonk?"

"Someone like you who comes to a hospital, plays games, has juice and crackers, and gets to go home at the end of the day, while the rest of us are prisoners here."

She smiled. Not because what he said was funny, but because in some subtle way his voice had softened. Although the handicapped boy did not smile back, he did

7

speak to her again. "My name is Christopher Hayden," he said, resting his chin on the edge of his pillow. "Called Kit."

"Jeannie West," she volunteered. "And I was part of that pilot program of Dr. Salk's vaccine. My uncle vaccinated me against polio with killed virus. That's why I can work here."

"Ah, your uncle. That must be Dr. Storey—young Martin—the boy genius and great white hope. He told me I'd be meeting you. So you come by all your bleeding-heart stuff naturally. How touching. And you'll grow up to be a nice sweet nurse who puts the needle in the bottom of all Dr. Storey's patients."

"I'm going to be a doctor," Jeannie said.

"Wonderful! Marvelous! You'll be a *doctor*, and I'll be the crip making potholders at the Goodwill workshop. And you've had vaccine, so you'll never get what I got. Nor will anyone else after this lousy year. How's that for lousy, stinking timing? Dr. Jonas Salk's going to wipe out polio, and I'm going to be left like this forever. Why me?"

Jeannie felt ill-equipped to handle this boy's self-pity, yet she didn't think that she could walk away. She thought if she showed some interest in him it might help calm him down. "How old are you?" she asked.

"Seventeen," he snapped grimly.

She examined his face, which was smooth and beardless. A light beading of perspiration ran along his forehead and up into his hairline, giving his head the sheen of a marble statue. "Fourteen?" she asked, calling his bluff.

"Seventeen," he repeated.

"Then you'd be in the adult ward. I'm fourteen."

Kit appeared to be sinking from his overwrought state into an unpleasant but more manageable mood. "Okay—

8

fourteen. Yeah, me, too. Listen, why don't you dump those games? You look stupid standing there hanging onto them."

Jeannie looked down. By now her arms were aching, but holding the boxes made her feel as if she were doing something official, even if she was only standing in aisle A talking to an angry boy. "I've got to give them out," she said.

"Okay. Goodbye."

Although he had dismissed her for a second time, she didn't feel inclined to go. What she really wanted to do was ask again if this boy was Yeti, whose voice was haunting her. But she did not repeat the question. There were at least half a dozen patients old enough to be writing those messages.

When she didn't leave, Kit glared at her. "Goodbye!" he repeated.

"Did anyone ever tell you that you're awfully hard to get along with?" she inquired.

"Me? Hard to get along with?"

"Yes. Kind of like a bull looking for a red cape."

"Oh my, Jeannie West—that's very poetic. The girl speaks in similes. So are you a poet as well as a doctor?"

Jeannie laughed. "A poet? I don't think so. I like to write. I mean—I'd like to join the newspaper when I start high school this fall. Well, I mean, I . . ."

Kit never let her finish. *"When* you start high school in the fall. How wonderfully simple. I'll give you a simile in return for yours. Well, girl, I'm like a newspaper that's been left too long in the rain. How's that for a simile?"

Jeannie nodded. His words made her look at his stretched-out body. *A newspaper left too long in the rain.* "How bad is it?" she asked, saying the first thing that came into her head. "How bad is your polio?"

"Not bad," he replied. "But, Doc—Dr. West—let me

tell you, Doc, I'm never going to be an All-American football player."

"Were you?"

"I don't know if you're for real or just wonky. No, I was not a football player. But I was starting to do some rock climbing, and I won't ever be able to do that again."

"I'm sorry, terribly sorry," she murmured. "What about your therapist—what does the therapist say?"

" 'Keep working, dammit. Keep working, dammit.' She has a very limited vocabulary."

"She talks like that? Just like a parrot?"

Kit laughed. "Like a parrot? Another simile—a comparison using 'like' or 'as'—but I prefer mine to be somewhat more original. But, hey, look out—here comes Old-Death-and-Dying."

Jeannie turned her head. There bustling toward them was a short, formidable-looking nurse. Despite what Kit had called her, Jeannie knew that the gray-haired nurse's name was Cabot.

Cabot closed in quickly. "Kit Hayden, are you still hanging around here? Mrs. Goldberger was expecting you in therapy twenty minutes ago."

"Well, I tried to hail a cab."

"You and your smart talk, boy. You weren't talking that way two weeks ago when you were so sick you didn't know where you were, and you wouldn't let go of my hand."

Kit scowled. Jeannie didn't have to be a mind reader to see that he didn't want Cabot discussing his illness.

"Who was supposed to take you? Alonzo? Alonzo, that good-for-nothing orderly. Lazy. Never where he's supposed to be."

"If you give me an oar, I'll paddle there myself," Kit said. "Or call me Popeye, give me a can of spinach, and I'll be strong enough to walk."

"Quiet. You're showing off. And, Miss West, the children are waiting for their games. You are disappointing them."

As Cabot was speaking, she flicked out one hand and spun the gurney around, catching both of them off guard. With unexpected force, Kit's head butted into Jeannie's arm. Boxes opened, checkers and crayons rolled, paper money floated through the air. In a few seconds, the aisle was too cluttered for Cabot to roll the gurney away.

"Oh, help," Jeannie gasped, falling to her knees. She'd made a mess. Cabot was furious. Kit was not getting to therapy. She felt like a fool.

Kit seemed to understand. "Allow me to be of assistance, madame," he said, swinging his arms off the end of the gurney as if he were some kind of mechanical robot who could whisk everything back into the right boxes.

"No funny stuff, boy," Cabot warned.

Jeannie began to scrape some of the cards and pieces together. She knew Kit was looking down at her. At that moment she was not feeling happy that their paths had crossed.

"Jeannie," he said, stretching out to steal some of the Monopoly cards she was holding.

"What?"

"I'll trade you Marvin Gardens for Boardwalk plus a ride on the Reading Railroad."

Looking up, Jeannie managed to find a small smile. "You and I seem to mix like oil and water," she said, offering him one more unoriginal simile.

Kit grinned a soft, crooked grin. "And Cabot and I mix like a pair of starved puppies tied in the same sack."

There was an awkward moment of silence. Jeannie broke it. "Yours was better than mine," she admitted.

"Of course," he said.

By now, Jeannie had cleared the way so Cabot could

move the gurney. Just as she was beginning to do so, Jeannie jumped to her feet. "Kit—Kit," she called, holding something out to him. "Didn't you say you'd lost a pencil?"

Looking fierce and resentful again, Kit grabbed it from her fingers. "How would you like to be so stinking helpless," he said, "that you can't pick up your own stinking pencil from the floor?"

2

$\mathcal{F}$OR DAYS following Jeannie's first meeting with Kit, his face was tense and angry whenever he glanced in her direction. When he spoke, he wouldn't look at her. Jeannie felt as if a thundercloud was poised above his head, ready to rain down on her if she came too close to where he lay.

Sometimes she watched him when he wasn't looking at her, but she gave up any idea of talking with him and concentrated on the younger children. They seemed eager for her company. As she got to know them, a lot of her awkwardness disappeared. Happy to be needed, she worked harder and harder.

When she came home exhausted, her mother asked whether she was eating enough and her father asked whether she was sure she didn't want to go away to camp with Lisabeth. Her sister, Jill, wouldn't leave her alone, either. Jill wanted more of her attention, yet Jill's ten-year-old concerns seemed suddenly petty compared to those of the children in the polio ward.

And then there was Yeti. She thought of Yeti as "he," even if she had no proof. Besides Kit, the only patient who appeared to possess any of Yeti's qualities was a quiet, secretive teenager named Trilby. As far as Jeannie was concerned, Trilby was some kind of plump vegetable growing in a fenced-off plot of ground. She wheeled silently about in her chair; she clumped by on new braces.

Sometimes she typed letters on a portable typewriter. She looked neither happy nor unhappy.

Although Trilby was a possibility, Jeannie hadn't eliminated Kit from suspicion. But she never saw him writing anything. Mostly, he lay on his back staring at the ceiling.

Jeannie had no clues, and still Yeti's messages kept appearing. His Fourth of July message was typical. Taped to the side of one of the iron lungs, it was the first thing she saw as she came into the ward. Usually, she avoided that area of the ward. Since the nurses spent so much time there, she was able to tell herself that she was needed more elsewhere.

That morning, though, Jeannie headed immediately toward the respirators. Biting down on her lower lip, she read what was printed on the lined paper. Then she read it through again.

> *condemned i am to live in the belly of an iron whale that wheezes and squeezes and measures my hours and will never cough me out and set me free. lonely i am, caught by ropes of rank kelp, trailing rainbow bubbles of air, as the whale frightens all away, leaving me drowning in a cold and friendless sea so huge that i am invisible for all time.*
>
> *YETI*

Because of Yeti's message, Jeannie spent the entire morning with the respirator patients. She told them stories, massaged necks, offered snacks.

In other parts of the ward, patients got stronger, sat up in wheelchairs, learned to use braces, and went home; but the lineup in the lungs was always the same. As Yeti said, these children were swallowed for all time. They had to live with paralysis and pain, with itches they could not scratch. They had difficulty talking, difficulty eating.

Jeannie shuddered at the idea of lives where improvement was not possible.

Strangely enough, however, she found that the lung patients tended to be optimistic. Like other polio kids, they talked of getting better, of getting out, of playing baseball again, even though it wasn't going to happen. While marveling at their spirits, she was still gripped by despair when she talked with them.

Depressed, she was straggling back toward the O.T. office when she ran into her Uncle Martin. As she worked on a holiday so the children wouldn't feel lonely, he paid hospital calls.

"You have the languid air of a lass who has spent a morning ministering to respirator patients," he said by way of a greeting.

"Yes," she answered, tucking her hair behind her ears.

"Did they tell you of their dreams of flying? There is something about those breathing machines—oxygen bubbles, perhaps—that seems to make them have fantastical dreams of planes and birds."

"Yeti dreams of flying."

"Oh, Yeti," Martin answered. "Is that mystery still being bruited about?"

Jeannie nodded. Being around her uncle, listening to him, improved her mood. "Yes, Yeti is still writing. But no one knows who he is."

Martin smiled. "Well, what would life be like without mystery? But listen, my little ballerina, I have a favor to ask. If you will—a favor which will require some amount of tact."

"What?" Jeannie said. She was never against doing favors for someone as special as Martin. He was handsome and so tall that he made her feel as if she *were* a little ballerina. "What can I do?"

"It concerns Master Kit Hayden."

Jeannie slumped back against the wall. "What about him?"

"There's to be a function this afternoon, a ceremonial luncheon in the common room for everyone in chairs or up on braces. Having him come would mean a world of Sundays to me. You see, he possesses this wondrous wheelchair, but he will not use it, except to go to physical therapy. Could you possibly dance about and weave a spell upon him? He's been having a rough time and needs, I think, a little jollying up."

Jeannie didn't want to refuse Martin, yet she hated to lay herself on the line for a project doomed to failure. "Well," she began hesitantly.

"Not 'well' but 'yes, Uncle Martin!' Why, you're a pretty wench and he's a growing boy. It's a holiday and the natives are restless, so put yourself out a bit. Help me, help Cabot, and we shall crown you queen of the May."

Slowly swallowing down a giggle at the way Martin spoke when he was warmed up, a way that would have been pompous if he didn't laugh at himself as he talked, Jeannie nodded. "I'll try. I really will. But can I ask you something, and will you answer me seriously?"

"Seriously."

"Is Kit Yeti?"

Martin shrugged. "Who knows? You may have to ask him that yourself as you are cajoling him to join the festivities."

Only a minute later, Jeannie found herself walking obediently toward aisle A. She didn't have any notion of what she was going to say when she got to Kit Hayden's bed; still, a promise was a promise.

By Kit's bedside, a portable radio was playing a baseball broadcast. Jeannie didn't know anything about baseball. Alonzo, the orderly that Cabot constantly accused of laziness, was mopping the floor under Kit's bed with elaborate care. Though the two of them were not talking, it was apparent that Alonzo's interest in clean floors increased in proximity to the radio.

"What's the score?" Jeannie asked, knowing that her question was mindless and the answer made no difference to her.

Kit didn't turn his head. He kept his eyes fixed on the ceiling as if it were a movie about Eskimos dressed in white battling in a snowstorm.

" 'Sa All-Star game," Alonzo answered cheerfully. "National's ahead two nothing." Then he tucked his mop under one arm, bent to lift Kit's wastebasket. "See you later, son," he said, patting Kit on the shoulder. "An' see if you can fix it for the fireworks." With those words, he shuffled off, leaving Jeannie alone with Kit.

She didn't have anything to say. She had no notion how she was going to persuade him to sit in his chair, much less get him to wheel down the hall to the luncheon. Instead of saying something, she did something. On impulse, she backed up and sat in his wheelchair.

She'd never been in a wheelchair before. It wasn't, she found, particularly comfortable. Her feet rested on two hard flaps. Her hips were squeezed by cold metal. At her sides, her hands hung uselessly. Curious, she lifted one hand and pulled at one of the wheels. The chair spun to the left. Now her back was turned to Kit. Absorbed, she took hold of both wheels and began to experiment with going backward and forward, turning from side to side. She wondered how it would feel to be confined, to live a life in a wheelchair, permanently substituting wheels for legs.

"That's my chair," Kit said after a while. His voice was hollow, reflecting no particular emotion.

"You're not using it," she replied, struggling to be as noncommittal as he was.

"I'm *thinking* of using it."

His tone of voice irritated her. "Possession is nine-tenths of the law, my father always says. And right now, I'm sitting here."

"Move it," he said.

"No," she answered.

She was angry at him for the way he treated her and other people. He waved his illness through the air, she decided, like a flag, expecting everyone to feel sorry for him.

Kit seemed to be intrigued by her new attitude. He rolled over on his side and propped himself up on one elbow. The radio droned on. "I bet," he said, speaking loud enough that she could hear him over the announcer's continuous monologue, "you think suffering makes people noble."

She rolled the chair up to the edge of his bed. Her own feet were heavy, leaden. "Maybe some people," she said, "but not you. You're like a bad boy who needs to be spanked."

Kit nodded thoughtfully. "And you," he said, after a very long pause, "are carrying your head between your shoulders like a beach ball you're afraid someone is going to bat away."

Jeannie laughed. *"What* does *that* mean?"

Kit laughed, too. "It means I know Martin Storey has sent you here to get me to come to the kiddie party down the hall."

Jeannie blushed guiltily. It was terrible to be so transparent.

"You look kind of pretty when you get hot and embarrassed," Kit said as he flicked off the radio.

"I feel . . . like a scarecrow with straw in all the wrong places," she mused.

Reaching out, Kit tapped the back of her left hand

with his. "Not bad," he said. "With a little practice, you may turn into a doctor-poet yet. I mean, one of us has to do something special in life."

Jeannie was listening, but she didn't look up. She hardly knew him, and she wasn't sure how to answer when he was so negative about his own future.

"Jeannie? Jeannie with the light-brown hair?"

"What?" she answered, suspicious as she heard his wheedling tone.

"I'll get in the chair and come to lunch for Uncle Martin if you'll do something for me. For a lot of others, too."

"Like what?" she asked.

"Well . . . Alonzo bought fireworks with his own money, fireworks that Cabot says we're not going to have tonight—fire hazard and a lot of other stinking arguments like that. If you get your uncle to get permission for fireworks on the roof tonight—in the garden there—then I'll throw myself in the chair and race you to lunch."

"That's bribery."

He shook his head. "No, a deal."

"I don't make deals," she said.

"You don't?" He was chuckling. "Then what do you call the arrangement you made with your silver-tongued uncle? Come on, girl, this isn't for me, you know. It's for the little ones. It's a holiday, remember? My family is coming this afternoon, but a lot of these kids don't have families in town to visit them. They need a lift."

Jeannie knew he was right. She thought his plan was wonderful, and she was sure that Martin could manage things. Martin could do anything. He had the whole hospital staff wrapped around his little finger. Besides, Martin wanted Kit up out of bed. "Okay, sure," she told him.

She stood up. Liberating herself from the chair improved her mood. She skipped and did little glissades in the aisle.

"She dances, too," Kit called out. "Look at her dance."

By the time she had turned back to him, Kit had already made the transfer from the bed to the wheelchair. She had been spared the discomfort of seeing whether his legs flopped uselessly as he negotiated the move. She was grateful but at the same time puzzled that he hadn't needed help. Even if he wasn't Yeti, his strangeness both fascinated and repelled her.

"See," he told her. "You won. I bet you're an older sister. Older sisters always win."

Jeannie was an older sister and she was used to winning, yet at this moment she didn't think that she'd won anything. That Kit was out of bed had little to do with her.

While she was thinking about this, he whizzed by her in his wheelchair, whipping it up the aisle. Pausing before little Karen, he snatched her up into his lap and turned the wheelchair in crazy careening circles in front of the nurses' station. Jeannie had never seen him use a chair before, but there he was, spinning around with great skill.

After a moment, he stopped and turned back to her. "You were dancing before. Are you a dancer?"

She shrugged uncomfortably. "Used to be," she admitted.

"Well, you don't look like one now. Right now you look like a cowgirl who has just discovered she has a rattlesnake creeping up to bite her."

Jeannie cocked her head and grinned. "I do," she told him. "And the rattlesnake's name is Kit."

3

OT LONG after the successful Fourth of July fireworks, Kit got crutches and leg braces. Since he wore the braces under pajamas and a robe, Jeannie could see very little of them. They were bolted to a stiff-looking pair of brown shoes, and Jeannie suspected that—like the ones on many of the patients—they came all the way up his legs and fastened at the waist.

Kit acted as if they didn't exist. The crutches gathered dust in the corner behind his bedside table. When Kit chose to get up and move about, he used the chair.

One Tuesday morning near the end of July, Kit rolled into the doorway of the common room when Jeannie was playing with Karen and Tooter. He stopped the chair at the threshold and left it there blocking the entrance. Although he pretended to read, Jeannie knew that he was watching her with the children. Despite the fact that he had expressed interest in the children by pleading for Alonzo's fireworks, he never made an effort to talk with them or play games of any kind. He just watched.

Without comment, Jeannie allowed him to sit there as she went on with the game she had devised for the children. Tooter was a seven-year-old with paralyzed legs. He was never going to walk normally. The best he could hope for, her uncle had told her, was some sort of clumsy, heaving gait, using crutches and elaborate braces with locked knees. Because being up on his feet was so difficult, Tooter preferred traveling by wheelchair. Much to the displeasure of Cabot and the rest of the hospital staff, he drove it as if it were a racing car.

Karen's condition was somewhat better. She was able to walk about, using braces and short crutches. Her balance wasn't good, but she had some working muscles in her legs, even if they were weak and shrunken from weeks of disuse. Jeannie held Karen lightly by the shoulders as she clomped across the room, then back again, as part of their game.

They were doing a picture puzzle. The puzzle was on a low table on one side of the room and the loose pieces were on the sill under the front window. Karen and Tooter had to negotiate the length of the room to select pieces and fit them in where they belonged.

For Tooter in his chair, the game was easy and fun. For Karen, it was another matter. Every step was a struggle. Her red curls bounced against her shoulders. She frowned and licked at her lips as she placed one foot in front of the other. When Jeannie suggested that Karen could sit down for a while and play the game from her wheelchair, she refused.

"No," she insisted, doing her best to stamp a foot held rigid by its metal brace. "Mrs. Goldberger and my mama say if I keep working, I can go home, and I want to go home!"

As soon as her speech had been made, Karen started across the room, holding another piece of the spotted giraffe. Silently Jeannie applauded the child's grit. From the corners of her eyes, she checked to see if Kit had been paying attention.

As she was thinking about Kit, Tooter accidentally looped his chair so it caught the edge of Karen's left crutch. Before Jeannie could help, Karen was down. Falls didn't usually rattle her, but this one was complicated by the fact that her crutch disconnected the tubing on Tooter's urine bag, spreading a dark-yellow stain over Karen and the linoleum floor.

"Oh, gosh," Tooter groaned. "But it was an accident. Oh, gosh—oh, I'm sorry. Oh, look ... Oh ..."

"Shush, Tooter," Jeannie told him, unsure of what to do. "She's all right. You're all right."

As she lifted a wet, dripping Karen to her feet, Jeannie looked around. "Kit," she called, swiveling her head toward the doorway. Kit had vanished. The doorway was empty. Karen, stoic Karen, was beginning to sob.

Jeannie was angry at herself. She had let the game get too wild.

"I didn't have an accident. It wasn't my accident," Karen cried. The stubbornness that made her keep walking when she was ready to drop from weariness made her refuse to appear in the ward in wet, stained clothes.

Karen began to howl while Tooter bounced up and down in his chair, continuing to apologize in increasingly loud tones.

Only then did Jeannie notice Trilby. Trilby was slouched in front of the TV in a high-backed chair in one corner of the room. Her legs in their braces spread like the sides of a wishbone. In her lap was a box of stationery and a pen. For a second Jeannie wondered again if fat, emotionless Trilby could be the suffering, sensitive Yeti, but she couldn't dawdle over this thought.

"Trilby," she pleaded, self-consciously aware that she had never spoken directly to the other girl before. "Look, I've made a mess here, and I need help. How about—I mean, would you look after these two just for a minute while I run for Cabot?"

Trilby's face showed nothing, not sympathy for the children or for Jeannie.

2 3

"Oh, Trilby," Jeannie begged. "Karen, look—I'll fetch Cabot and dry clothes and . . ."

"Yes, of course," Trilby said, interrupting softly. Her face was still blank, yet her voice had a surprisingly musical quality.

Grateful, Jeannie ran to find Cabot. While Jeannie explained, the stocky nurse made her cringe by staring at her with little squirrel eyes. Jeannie knew she thought that Martin Storey's niece was a nuisance to the hospital staff.

"I'll clean up the floor," Jeannie volunteered, anxious to redeem herself.

Cabot shook her head. "Alonzo's job. He's probably goldbricking somewhere, listening to another ball game with Kit. That's where he always is when he's supposed to be working."

Feeling relieved that this catastrophe was about to be over, Jeannie decided to organize a checkers tournament for the afternoon. Cabot would be pleased if she paired up older and younger children so no one was left out. She was beginning to arrange the teams when she realized that Cabot, still annoyed, was speaking to her.

"Miss West, are you there? I've just remembered that Mrs. Goldberger wants to see you in P.T.—the Physical Therapy room, that is."

"When?" Jeannie asked. No one could work in Hanover without hearing about Sylvia Goldberger, the terrible-tempered therapist. Jeannie had never met her. Now she felt as if Cabot was sending her to P.T. for punishment and not because the doctor had really asked to see her.

"Any time, she said, so why don't you hightail it up there and give us a little peace around here for a while?"

2 4

Jeannie wanted to cry. This was another one of the days when she wondered what she was doing in a hospital and if she would ever be strong enough to become a doctor.

"Now!" Cabot repeated.

"But . . ." Jeannie said, "she may be with a patient and—"

"Take your longfellows directly to P.T. She'll let you know if she doesn't want you."

Any further delay simply meant more scolding from Cabot, so Jeannie turned and headed toward the elevator. The P.T. room was up on four. It would be easy to find because the linoleum blocks on the floor were inlaid with colored footprints. The red ones led to the front door, the yellow to the cafeteria, the pink to Pediatrics, green to X-ray, and blue to Dr. Goldberger's room. The footprints even stepped into the elevator and out again on the appropriate floor.

Reluctantly, Jeannie followed the blue ones to the P.T. room. There, taped to the door, was a message from Yeti.

marbles, she says, keep picking up marbles with your fingers and with your toes, and we will strengthen living muscle fibers to learn the work of dead ones, because marbles are the passport to being whole and free from that prison of a body. does she know, can she know as she rolls color-swirled marbles over my brain that i dream of escape, that i dream i shall walk free of this place, free from disease to a high, shining world where i can walk with strong, fine legs and with a head full of clouds and emptied of spinning marbles?

YETI

Jeannie's head was full of Yeti's words as she peered through the window in the door into the therapy room. She saw a thin woman with dark hair wound into a coronet of braids about her head. The woman wore a red dress and an oversized white lab coat. She was helping a boy work his way across a pair of parallel bars.

There was other equipment in the room, most of it strange and unfamiliar to Jeannie. Down at the far end, Dr. Goldberger's assistants helped two girls on something that looked like a combination of a seesaw and a rowing machine.

Jeannie tapped lightly, hoping she wouldn't be noticed and could head back to the ward. Yeti's message with its vision of freedom in a high, shining world was still bothering her.

To her disappointment, Dr. Goldberger heard the tapping and beckoned for her to come in. Slowly, Jeannie turned the knob and entered. While pulling her shoulders back, she managed to produce some semblance of a smile.

"Hi, Jeannie," called the boy, whose name was Donald. "Want to see me on the bars? I can walk. Watch!"

Donald's enthusiasm relaxed her a little. Then Dr. Goldberger spoke. "Good day," she said.

Jeannie stiffened again. The woman hardly came up to Jeannie's shoulder, but her voice was authoritative, with a pronounced German accent.

"Is it always *Jeannie*?" Dr. Goldberger asked.

"Pardon?" the girl asked, confused by the question.

"What is your given name? Your full name?"

"Jeanne-Marie West," she managed to reply.

"Good. That sounds proper. I shall call you Jeanne-Marie."

"See how good I am, Jeannie?" Donald asked, interrupting. "See me."

While Jeannie was answering, Dr. Goldberger whisked the boy from the bars. In a minute she had him back in his chair and rolling out of the room as she informed him in her staccato voice that he had worked hard, could do better the next day, and she was going to speak with Jeanne-Marie.

Sylvia Goldberger leaned against her desk. She wasn't a pretty woman in any particular way, Jeannie decided, yet there was a sense of motion about her that made her seem beautiful. Jeannie found herself wishing that she was small and vivid instead of tall, colorless, and gawky.

"I have asked you to come," Dr. Goldberger informed her, "because of Christopher Hayden."

Jeannie frowned.

"So what is it, my girl, that is such a deal about that request? Martin—your uncle—tells me that over Christopher you have some influence."

"Only when he *wants* something. Then he's sweet as ice cream, and as cold. No, I only have influence when he's in a good mood. Everything has to be *his* way."

Dr. Goldberger smiled as if Jeannie had said something enormously amusing. "Yes, I have had that experience with him, too. The easiest of persons he is not. And he is not making the desired progress. He could, you know, go home, but I and his family prefer to have him remain until we can overcome this attitude and make him reach his potential."

"What is his potential?"

Dr. Goldberger removed a long hairpin and used it to secure her braids more firmly. "A very good prognosis for one leg. The other, with some surgery, will I should think function with a minimal brace. Yet, if he will not struggle, he will languish as a crippled person."

"But I don't understand. What do you think I can do?"

"It is my desire that you encourage him to apply effort to his program of physical therapy."

"Terrific," Jeannie answered. "And he'll say I sound just like you."

Amused again, Dr. Goldberger wrinkled her forehead. "So what is it he says I say?"

Jeannie knew she was going too far, but she said exactly what she was thinking. She mimicked Kit mimicking the therapist. " 'Keep working, dammit. Keep working, dammit.' "

Dr. Goldberger laughed softly. "Well, with the older of my patients, my vocabulary is not modified quite the way it tends to be with the younger ones. So answer now, will you try?"

Jeannie felt trapped. Trapped because she liked this woman, was responding to the warmth under the businesslike exterior. She also knew that any favor done for the therapist was going to please her uncle.

"Well, all right . . . yes," she agreed. "But I don't think it will work."

"We have exhausted, I think, all other avenues, and as you know, Christopher is an interesting but difficult boy."

This assessment of Kit encouraged Jeannie to ask a question. "Dr. Goldberger, is he Yeti?"

Sylvia Goldberger slid off the desk and smoothed out her lab coat. "If you do not know," she answered brusquely, "I do not suppose anyone does. Someone is taping up Yeti's messages. If it is not you, Jeanne-Marie, then Christopher is most probably not the Yeti, since that boy hardly speaks with another soul except you."

Knowing that the discussion was finished, Jeannie said goodbye, let herself out the door, and headed down the hall.

Someone was blocking her way. Someone in a wheelchair with a pair of crutches resting across its padded arms. Kit.

"So they've been at you again. Young Dr. West is supposed to make poor little Kit Hayden walk again. It's like a bad soap opera."

"You're right," Jeannie said, looking down at him and beginning to realize how angry she was at him and at being used to influence him.

"You look like a kettle of soup that's just about to boil over," he commented accurately.

Jeannie scowled. "Well, you look like a jack-in-the-box who refuses to pop up when they play 'Pop Goes the Weasel.' "

"I'm going to have to think about that one," Kit told her.

"Well, well," he said when she did not respond. "Now that you're on my case, can you cure me, Doc? I'm not March-of-Dimes-poster cute like little Karen on her braces, but you must have a few well-chosen words for me."

"I do," Jeannie said. " 'Keep working, dammit. Keep working.' "

Then, without waiting for his reaction, she strode off down the hall.

4

$\mathcal{S}$UMMER was almost over, but the polio epidemic raged on. Because a few children had caught polio from a bad batch of vaccine, the Salk inoculations had been suspended. Martin Storey assured Jeannie that the problem would be solved soon, that the program would be resumed, yet meanwhile new patients kept coming from Isolation to fill the beds in the pediatric ward.

Despite Jeannie's concern over the continuing numbers of young victims, she managed to maintain a tenuous friendship with Kit. Sometimes she remembered her talk with Dr. Goldberger, yet she never asked Kit to stand up and walk with his braces. Instead, she encouraged him until he agreed to help her work with the younger children. If he was in a good mood, he'd try to make them laugh by imitating Popeye. Though he tended to be too brusque, he seemed to enjoy being with them.

He and Jeannie were seldom alone. It was easier that way. Then Kit didn't seem so moody, didn't get so defensive. When they were by themselves, she frequently felt as if he were a porcupine poised to shoot quills in her direction.

Often, Jeannie asked Trilby to join them. Although the other girl spoke only in answer to a direct question, Jeannie continued to make an effort. Trilby was still in the hospital because she had had an operation to fuse the bones in her left ankle. If there was pain, she never spoke of it. Nor did she ever complain of loneliness, even though her parents—who lived on a ranch near Mt. Shasta —seldom visited.

Kit's family, on the other hand, came every Wednesday afternoon like some perfect TV family—father, followed by mother, followed by Kit's beautiful sister, Eleanor. They brought food and books. They made conversation. Jeannie never talked with Kit when they were there, but she watched enough to see that Kit did not seem to have very much to say to them.

Only the day before, by the drinking fountain, Jeannie had accidentally come face to face with Eleanor, a confident sixteen-year-old who wore pastel headbands on her pale blond hair. She was much shorter than Jeannie. First she had examined Jeannie's apron. Then, in a casual yet friendly way she'd said, "Well, Jeannie West—I've been hearing about you."

Eleanor's words and glossy manner had made Jeannie nervous, so that all she'd managed was a mumbled statement about being expected in the P.T. room.

Thinking about Kit and his family, about Trilby and hers, Jeannie clutched a stack of new-patient charts and began following the blue footprints to deliver them to Dr. Goldberger.

Preoccupied as she was, she almost missed Yeti's message. It was taped above the drinking fountain where she and Eleanor had been talking only the day before.

why me, god, why me? life isn't fair, i know, yet why have i been chosen to suffer, to lumber through life graceless as a bear? when i leave this white cave of protection, naked and exposed, i shall have to limp from day to year, a freak for the curious to stare at and the compassionate to shower with unwanted pity and attention. then, too, the jealousy

*will never go away, jealousy of all who are straight
and strong and free, the unmarked who can blithely
skim through weeks and years with no thought of
the miraculous wholeness they possess.*

YETI

As Jeannie caught the elevator and hurried on toward
the P.T. room, she was suddenly aware that her step was
light and dancelike compared with Yeti's description of
his own bearlike lumbering.

Turning a corner, she forgot Yeti as she found Kit
splayed out on the floor on his stomach. Standing over
him was Sylvia Goldberger. Instead of pajamas and a
robe, Kit was wearing gym shorts and a T-shirt. His legs
were encased in their braces. The crutches were lying
where they'd fallen. His left leg, she saw immediately,
was pitifully thin. The braces she had never seen on the
legs she had never looked at were heavy, complicated con-
traptions with hinges at the knee joints.

Almost unconsciously, Jeannie flattened herself against
the wall. Kit would be humiliated if he knew she was
staring at him. She wished there were some way to slink
back to the ward without having to admit to Cabot that
the charts were undelivered.

Neither Kit nor Dr. Goldberger had noticed her yet.
They were too involved in their own confrontation. The
doctor had her hands on her hips, and she was gazing
down at Kit without making any effort to help him to his
feet. "Get up," she was telling him. "Pick yourself up,
Christopher."

"I am not going to get up."

"Get up, Christopher," she repeated.

Two Pink Ladies came down the hall at that moment
wheeling a magazine cart. They had to scrape the wall
in order to get by. Jeannie saw them shaking their heads

as Dr. Goldberger told Kit once again that he must pick himself up. The women were sorry for him, believed someone should bend down and lift him to his feet. Jeannie was confused. If it had been Donald or Karen on the floor, she would have rushed to help.

"Christopher, my boy, you are trying my patience. Now draw up your right knee, use your hands and pull—using the crutches—until you are back on your feet."

"I'm not going to do it."

"You are."

Kit shook his head. "I am not going to get up," he said, speaking entirely without passion. "Alonzo can sweep me off into the garbage, but I am not going to walk. I am never going to walk again."

"You are going to rise and walk if we two have to stay here until hell freezes over. Just look at you—if you cannot be some kind of star athlete, you do not want to walk, you will not struggle. For you, it's wings or nothing!"

Kit groaned. "Oh, no—not that again."

"Yes, that again. There is in this culture something deficient. It makes boys with wings and girls with roots, when we all need *both*. Not everyone, Christopher, can fly all the time. You must put down roots to help you heal from this polio."

Kit propped himself on his elbows to answer this speech. It was then that he caught sight of Jeannie. "What are you cowering there for?" he asked, looking relieved to have some distraction. "Wings and roots, roots and wings. I'm not sure what she means, but it's quite a show you're watching, Jeannie. And me—I feel like the man on the flying trapeze who's just missed the bar and discovered that they've forgotten to put up the net."

Jeannie stepped forward. She ignored the metaphor about wings as she tried to match Kit's circus simile with one of her own. "I . . . I feel like I'm watching a lion who hasn't been fed for days and is waiting for someone stupid enough to walk into his cage."

Dr. Goldberger squinted amiably as she listened to this exchange. But she didn't make any comment.

Turning to Dr. Goldberger and trying not to look ill at ease, Jeannie said, "I have some charts for you. Shall I leave them on your desk?"

"Yes," the doctor answered. "Now, Christopher, my friend, it is time for you to stop imitating a floor mop and get to your feet."

Kit didn't move. Jeannie did. Eager for a chance to escape, she edged past them. Kit chose that moment to call out to her. "Jeannie, wait! I have something to ask you. Wait."

As she spun around, she half expected to see him on his feet rushing after her, but he was sprawled in the same position on the floor. "Jeannie, would you like to start a newspaper—for the children? With stories, cartoons? There must be a mimeograph somewhere in this fortress where we can run it off."

Tugging at the bib of her apron, Jeannie choked back an impulse to laugh at the odd fact that Kit had chosen to offer this suggestion while he was lying on the floor at Dr. Goldberger's feet.

After a moment or two, Jeannie answered. "Sure. Why not?"

"Jeannie West is a poet," Kit told Sylvia Goldberger with a funny grin on his face.

Jeannie sighed. "Very funny. Cabot would say 'My feet show it—they're longfellows!' Well, I'm not a poet, but . . . well . . . meet me in the common room and we'll talk about a paper. But I've got to get back now. Got to clean up some fingerpaints before Cabot finds them, be-fore she takes my head off."

Then she gave him a little wave. She'd discuss the possibility of a newspaper, after he figured out how to get away from Dr. Goldberger.

About twenty minutes later, as she was swabbing up the last of the slimy paints, Kit wheeled in to find her. His crutches were slung back across the armrests. The gym shorts had been replaced by pajamas and his plaid robe. His hair was damp and plastered against his head. Jeannie wondered if Kit had lost the battle of wills, if he had picked himself up and walked back to the P.T. room.

"About the newspaper," she began, feeling self-conscious as she remembered the scene she had watched. "Let's make some plans. Maybe Trilby will help. She's got a typewriter, too."

"Later," Kit said.

"Why not now? I'll do some writing for it. Will you?"

Kit shook his head. "Not me," he insisted solemnly. "I'm not a writer. I'll be publisher. But later."

"What's wrong with now?"

"We're going to take a field trip first and find a mimeograph machine."

Jeannie tossed the last of the rainbow-smudged rags into a small basin. "A field trip? What's wrong with just asking?"

Kit shook his head. "Too easy. I don't like doing things the easy way."

"So I've noticed," Jeannie observed.

Kit was too absorbed in his idea to react to her tone. "Anyone who wants to can come and join us," he declared. "In chairs or on crutches—we'll have a parade. A mutiny. And I have money. We can even follow the yellow feet to the cafeteria, and I'll treat everyone to milk shakes."

Because it was changeover time for the nursing staff, Cabot didn't see what was happening until her patients were long gone. There were nine of them, including

Jeannie and Alonzo, who had been persuaded to come help with the elevator doors. It was easy to entice Karen, Tooter, and a few of the others. Even Trilby consented to accompany them. They settled on wheelchairs as the fastest means of escape.

As they wheeled along, they waved and smiled at people. Because Karen requested it, they made a stop at the nursery, where through two sets of glass doors they got a fleeting look at babies lying like hot dogs wrapped in white buns. Then some Cabot-like nurse shooed them off, and they headed for Admitting.

There, after finding the sought-after mimeograph, they weighed themselves on the wheel-on scale. Karen giggled when Kit insisted that her chair weighed seventy-five pounds and she a mere seven.

Jeannie had reservations about the adventure, but the others—with the exception of the sphinx-faced Trilby—were laughing and having a wonderful time.

After Admitting, they went up to the roof garden, where they sang "God Bless America" for the old people and post-surgical patients who were sitting in the sun. With the help of an agreeable young technician, they stopped at X-ray and peered at all the complicated machines. Cabot was forgotten, the polio ward was forgotten. All they had on their minds was driving their chairs to new destinations.

To Jeannie's amazement, no one asked why they were out of the ward. She began to realize that the hospital staff enjoyed seeing the wheelchair kids enjoying themselves. Besides, her apron and Alonzo's green uniform seemed to give the expedition some kind of official sanction.

Once they had toured and filled their stomachs with chocolate milk shakes, Kit came up with another unlikely suggestion. "Let's go out," he said. "Let's take a little spin around the block."

And there they were—Alonzo, Jeannie, and seven kids in wheelchairs out taking a spin when Cabot, Martin Storey, and a sallow nurse called Frenchy came running along the sidewalk in pursuit.

Immediately, all spinning ceased. Trilby looked as if she were going to throw up. Several of the kids started to cry. Alonzo's slouch became almost a crouch. Jeannie started to perspire profusely. Only Kit did not appear to be distressed.

"Alonzo! Jeannie, what is going on?" Cabot demanded.

"See, Mrs. Cabot, ma'am," Alonzo began in his quiet, shambling way. "Seemszat the children, they . . ."

"We're starting a newspaper," Jeannie said, aware that her silly explanation was not going to satisfy anyone. "We were looking for a mimeograph machine."

Tooter started to snicker, then Cabot shot him a menacing look.

"Jeannie, my little ballerina," Uncle Martin said, "I find it understandable that you wish everyone to have a rousing time, yet I think—"

Whatever Martin Storey thought, he never had a chance to say it. Before he finished his statement, something happened. Kit, taking hold of his crutches, rose up out of his wheelchair.

With an ungainly stride, he swung himself forward. His progress was slow and precarious. Though it seemed as if he were going to fall, he stayed upright.

"Dr. Storey," he said, breathing hard from his exertion. "It wasn't her fault or Alonzo's. It was my idea, sir, and they came because of me."

No one moved or said a word. Not one of them had ever seen Kit up on his feet before.

"What's the matter here?" Kit said, finally turning around and acknowledging the shocked silence. "You're as quiet as a flock of tongueless sheep."

Jeannie was listening, but she was looking, too. She was surprised to see that Kit was shorter than she. She was also surprised to find that she wanted to rush forward and give him a hug, but she didn't. Shyly, she hung back.

"Tongueless sheep," Kit repeated, prompting her.

Kit was on his feet because he wanted to be there, not because of any deal. Jeannie smiled at him. "Or," she suggested at last, "as quiet as a pack of barkless Basenji hounds."

5

By AUGUST 29, the second issue of the newspaper was finished and run off on the mimeograph machine in Admitting. Thinking about the paper, Jeannie slid into the breakfast nook, where Jill and her parents were waiting for her. As proof that the summer was ending, there was no morning fog outside, and sun streamed in. The beginning of school was only a few days away. In addition, Kit was going home.

She was happy for him but uncertain. This year, he would not be going to school. He was going to be tutored at home and taken to Hanover three days a week to continue therapy with Dr. Goldberger. Though Jeannie would keep helping in the ward, she'd only be there on Saturdays. She wondered whether she and Kit would still be friends when she was at Jackson High and they were not seeing each other five days a week.

A sharp little elbow was digging into her ribs. It was ten-year-old Jill. Turning, Jeannie looked at the girl as if she hadn't seen her for three months. "Gee, I know you," she teased. "I think my mother introduced us. And, wow, have you gotten tall. Watch out or you'll become a giant like me."

" 'Great oaks from little acorns grow,' " Jeannie's father remarked, looking over his paper. "And personally, I'm very fond of oaks."

Jeannie smiled at him and at her mother, who was

staring thoughtfully at her from behind a pair of horn-rimmed glasses, which, as usual, were slipping down the bridge of her nose. Her father was a dentist, the kind who asked you what you were planning to do with the rest of your life, then jammed his huge hands, two sponges, and a drill into your mouth, pretending to understand when you tried to answer. Her mother, calm and orderly, worked as his bookkeeper. Jeannie knew she had not seen enough of them lately. Or of Jill, either.

As Jeannie was thinking about her sister, the younger girl spoke up. "Only a week and we're going to get Jeannie back. That place won't be eating her up any more."

Smiling, Jeannie poured herself some cornflakes. She had spent the summer as preoccupied with the hospital as she had once been with ballet. Her parents, she knew, were concerned, as Jill had said, that the hospital was swallowing her. They had probably even spoken about this with her uncle. But they had never interfered.

With their silent support, she had done a good job in the post-polio ward, although she often felt she had gotten more from the children than she had been able to give. Today, however, was going to be a day of giving back. She was putting on a party for the whole ward. It would also be a going-away surprise for Kit.

Her mother's wire shopping cart was filled with paper hats, horns, streamers, popcorn she'd popped, cupcakes she'd baked. In addition, she had arranged with Mary Markham in Occupational Therapy to show some of Kit's beloved Popeye cartoons. Both Kit and the children would enjoy them. Some of the younger ones even called Kit "Popeye" because he liked to display the new arm muscles he was developing from using crutches. " 'I yam what I yam, and that's all that I yam,' " he liked to tell them.

Yes, she was thinking a little later, as she bounded up the hospital ramp, dragging the cart behind her, Kit was up using his crutches and braces instead of a chair. That was how he had won permission to go home. And he would probably walk out of the hospital without ever telling her if he was Yeti.

When she was upstairs heading toward the ward, she ran into her uncle standing by the utility closet talking with Alonzo.

"Some pennant race, eh, Doc?" the older man was saying while he leaned heavily on his mop.

"Exciting, yes. Can't say, however, I'd be disappointed if the Yankees are victorious. But I must admit, Alonzo, this summer I am not obsessed with sports but with the polio children—these who we all hope shall be the last." Martin put one arm lightly on Jeannie's shoulder to include her in the conversation, yet his words were still directed at Alonzo.

Alonzo lunged idly after a dustball. " 'Stoo many of them. 'Stoo many little crippled kids."

"Yes, but we are putting an end to that with Dr. Salk's vaccine and the one being worked on by Dr. Sabin. We are, as I keep telling every soul who will listen, going to KO polio. We are going to knock it out for all time!"

"I hope so," Jeannie answered fervently.

"We shall," her uncle replied. "Now, Red Riding Hood, for a shift in topic—where are you trundling with all the goodies? You'd best beware of big-eyed wolves."

"Oh, Uncle Martin," Jeannie laughed. "You're so funny. That's why everyone loves you."

"Everyone?" Martin Storey said, cocking an eyebrow. "Well, Mrs. Cabot may be an exception to that—especially since I interceded to parole the whole lot of you after that outrageous parade down the block."

At the mention of Cabot, Alonzo picked up his bucket and mop. Without saying goodbye, he trudged off slowly down the hall.

"Mrs. Cabot is a fine nurse, Jeannie my young colt. For all her glaring faults, Old-Death-and-Dying does a world of good."

Jeannie grinned. "Old-Death-and-Dying—Kit calls her that, too. How come? Why?"

When Martin answered her, it was with reluctance, as if he were giving away a secret. "Well, let me put it this way—she is a marvel with the truly sick, the ones we fear are going to perish in the night. She babied Kit for days upstairs when he was critical. Yet whenever she sees someone leaping toward health, Old-Death-and-Dying loses interest. Thus, as you see here in this ward—the scourge."

"If she's so good with those very sick ones, why isn't she still upstairs in Isolation?"

"A good question with a complex answer. Hospital politics, a rotation of shifts, and, besides, she has developed a special affinity for respirator patients. They are sick enough to require her sympathy and massive energy."

Jeannie understood more about Cabot, but at the same time she understood something about herself. She still spent more of her time on the children getting well than she did on the helpless ones in the lungs. She didn't tell her uncle what she was thinking. Perhaps she didn't have to, since he seemed to have a way of reading people's minds.

Besides, at that moment, something else claimed her attention. Kit, dressed in T-shirt and gym shorts, turned down the hall, following the blue footprints to the elevator on his way up to therapy. His back was toward them, so Jeannie could stare, examining how he was getting along.

Once he had abandoned the chair, he insisted on going everywhere on his feet. His right leg looked almost perfect. It had only a small brace on it, but the left one was clumsy. Although the knee joint worked, the lower leg was flaccid. To walk, Kit had to lean on his crutch, throw the foot forward, and ease his weight on it. Sometimes he lost his balance and fell. Getting up made him swear and grunt, yet he refused all help. He was definitely getting better.

"So he is going home today," Martin commented, "and someone I know is feeling a touch of sadness?"

Jeannie lowered her head. "Mmm . . . well, yes—but I've got this party to set up while he's at P.T. Will you come?"

"I'll pop in if I can. But, you know, you might also respectfully request Cabot's presence."

Jeannie did as he had suggested. Cabot proved to be helpful, too. Maybe she was simply glad to be getting rid of Kit, but she did dress and assemble the children. She got Alonzo to set up the projector. By the time Kit made his way back from his hour with Mrs. Goldberger, the children were gathered in the darkened common room. It was Cabot who volunteered to tell Kit that he was wanted there.

"Trilby says it's something about the crossword for the paper," the gray-haired nurse lied comfortably.

"Surprise," Jeannie and the children shouted as Kit hauled himself through the doorway.

He swayed there for a moment, then corrected his balance and gestured jauntily at them with one crutch. "Well, look at this. And it must even be legal because Cabot's in on it."

Something about Kit's casual acceptance of the fuss about to be made over him caused Jeannie to feel nervous. Examining his face, she guessed that he was simply putting on a performance. He didn't approve. He wasn't happy, but he wasn't going to spoil the fun for the children.

Jeannie had arranged for the movies to be first and the food afterward, so Alonzo wasted no time in getting the projector spinning. Kit propped himself in one corner, leaning against a radiator.

The cartoons flashed on the screen. With the exception of Trilby, who appeared to be writing letters in the dark, the children were all laughing and cheering. After waiting impatiently for a few minutes, Jeannie made her way back to where Kit stood. She leaned against the radiator next to him.

"Sorry," she said.

He didn't look at her. He stared forward at the flickering movie screen as if he hadn't heard her. At last, quietly, he answered. "For what?"

"For spoiling your last day by doing something that embarrasses you."

"Sshh!" hissed some of the children, annoyed by the sound of her whispering voice.

"Let's go out for a minute," Kit suggested, heaving himself toward the door.

Once outside the common room, they leaned silently against the wall near the drinking fountain. Finally Kit spoke. "I'm not angry," he told her, speaking in a soft voice. "Just unaccustomed. Unaccustomed to have anyone think I deserve anything special."

"But your family?"

"They don't find me special," he commented bitterly, "except in bad ways, like being specially moody or specially crippled."

Jeannie didn't know what to say. Kit never spoke about his family.

4 4

"You," he said, after another long pause, "and your uncle, Dr. Goldberger—even Cabot—are the first people ever, and I'm not mad. I'm sad. Sad to be leaving. Alonzo, too."

Jeannie's throat was giving her a problem. She felt as if it had a peach pit stuck in it. Instead of looking at Kit, she stared across the corridor at a mural of Pinocchio.

"I hope," he continued, "to see you on the outside. I hope that you won't—like Cabot—lose interest when I'm not sick." His words came out more and more slowly as he groped for what he wanted to say. "I feel, Jeannie, as if I'm a snake who has wriggled out into the sunlight, and I'm afraid of slithering back where it's dark and cold."

Jeannie didn't want to trade similes with him, but she thought she should offer something. "I feel," she said tentatively, "like a dancer who is . . ." Her voice trailed off when she was unable to dredge up a suitable comparison.

Kit's eyes widened. "You said once that you used to dance, but you never talk about it."

"No . . ." Her tone was wistful, giving away too much, she thought.

"So why don't you dance now? Why did you decide to become Dr. Curie instead of Margot Fonteyn?" Despite the familiar sarcasm in his voice, Jeannie didn't mind. It might save them both from the emotional scene toward which they had been heading. "So why *don't* you dance?"

Jeannie seldom gave an honest answer to that question, but Kit required one. "Because I grew too tall. Because my back is not flexible enough. They dismissed me, got rid of me. Oh, there was a more polite explanation, but classical ballet is a serious business, and I don't have the right body."

Reaching out, Kit pulled at her shoulder, turning her so they were facing one another. "Are you serious?"

"Of course, I'm serious."

"I always wondered," Kit said, speaking more to himself than to her, "why you understand."

Jeannie was puzzled. "What are you talking about?"

Reaching down, Kit eased a party hat and horn out of her hand. "It's simple enough," he told her, snapping the hat onto his head. "You understand *us* because you've been there, too. Feeling handicapped. Your body will keep you from being a great dancer as mine will keep me from being a great mountain climber."

"But . . ." she began, wanting to explain that she did not consider herself handicapped.

"Quiet," he warned, as he put the paper horn into his mouth and blew a single ear-splitting blast. "A party-horn help you have been." Then, tipping his hat, he began limping back toward the common room.

"Kit," she called out after him. She was touched by what he had said. Touched yet curious. She still wanted to know if he was Yeti.

"What?" he barked gruffly.

Jeannie swallowed down her question. "Nothing," she said, with a shrug. "Let's go back to the party."

The rest of the morning went by much too quickly. Everyone loved the popcorn and cupcakes. Martin Storey came. So did Dr. Goldberger. Jeannie never had time for another word with Kit. Before she knew it, the party was over, and his family was there, helping him pack up his things.

Jeannie wanted to promise Kit just one more time that they would see each other "outside." They didn't live far from one another, so that would be easy. She was plotting how she could tell him this when she encountered Eleanor Hayden weighing herself on the balance scale by the nurses' station.

4 6

"Hello," Eleanor said in a bright, glossy manner that made Jeannie wish for a magic carpet to whisk her away. The older girl was wearing a coral-colored angora sweater with a blue-and-coral plaid skirt.

"Hello," Jeannie replied, beginning to see that she was not going to have any chance to speak with Kit.

Eleanor looked into Jeannie's face. "Are you Kit's girl friend?"

"Girl friend?" Jeannie cried. "Me?"

Then she made a feeble excuse and fled to the O.T. room, where she stayed until she was sure that the Haydens had left. When she finally came back to the ward, she was determined to do something for the lung patients. She would take them horns, hats, and cupcakes so they could have their own party.

Kit's bed, she noticed, was already stripped. His wheelchair was gone. His wastebasket empty.

Trilby was sitting in her chair near aisle A with a stationery box in her lap. "I waited for you," she told Jeannie, "because I think he left something behind."

Jeannie looked up with surprise. Trilby had never spoken to her first. "Left something?"

"A note, maybe . . ."

"And you waited? Thank you, Trilby. Gee—thanks. I . . ."

Her voice trailed off as her eye caught sight of a piece of paper taped to the end of what had been, for two and a half months, Kit's bed. She wanted to run and snatch it up, but she also wanted to show Trilby that she appreciated her effort.

"Trilby—soon, when you go home, will you give me your address? I mean, we could write to each other, you and I. Would you like that?"

"Yes, I would." Trilby's voice was sweet as a wind chime.

47

Wondering why she had never pressed harder to understand the music inside Trilby, Jeannie gave the girl a warm smile. Then, when she could stand it no longer, she excused herself and hurried off to find Kit's note. It was on white paper, written in pencil in tiny printing.

forces move us, shape our lives for reasons we do not know and cannot hope to understand. like a great riptide we get carried along toward a distant shore where, slithering up on the sand, we shall grow legs and struggle toward new territory, which may be dark, fearful, and full of dangers. but, with strength, we crawl on, never questioning, because every once in a while a dancing flower pushes up between the weeds and astonishes with its fresh grace and beauty.

YETI

Jeannie stood there reading and rereading the message, straining to see it through her tears.

Fall 1956

6

EANNIE wondered if she had been the only one who had noticed the monarch butterfly hovering near the fir tree, then streaking off into the bright September morning. Turning, she examined Lisabeth walking in step with her toward Jackson High. Lisabeth, oblivious to something as small as a butterfly, was chattering about the first day of school. She was excited that she and Jeannie had finally left the lowly rank of freshmen to take their places as comfortable sophomores.

"'A sophomore is a wise fool,'" Jeannie commented. "Uncle Martin told me. From the Greek he studied in college."

If Lisabeth Richman was fascinated by this piece of unrequested scholarship, she didn't show it. She had her attention focused on two subjects she found equally fascinating—Algebra 2 and boys. Lisabeth was a nice little package, Jeannie thought, looking down at the other girl's glossy black hair and at her blue eyeglass frames, which lifted at the outside corners like dragonfly wings.

Jeannie and Lisabeth had been best friends since they had been room monitors in the sixth grade. Last year, to fortify themselves against the terror of being ninth-graders in a big high school, they had formed a tighter team than ever. They had both danced in the B troupe of the Modern Dance Club. On the *Jackson Banner*, they'd slaved away at traditional freshman jobs of typing, assembling sports statistics, and helping with last-minute rewrites.

Now they were together after spending another summer apart. Lisabeth had been a junior counselor at her old camp near Tahoe, where she had discovered boys. Jeannie, meanwhile, had worked another summer at Hanover Hospital.

Because of the Salk vaccine, available again in quantities large enough to protect everyone, there were no new polio cases. Jeannie's old ward—Cabot's territory—was being used for acute burn patients and children with leukemia or congenital diseases. Only a few respirators and a handful of post-polio kids, who had returned for corrective surgery on crippled legs or feet, served as an ongoing reminder of the terrible disease that had preoccupied her the summer before.

Trying to ignore the distance she sensed between Lisabeth and herself, she spoke up. "This year, I'm going to be more outgoing. Get to know more people."

Lisabeth nodded. "Me, too. But I've made up my mind. I *am* going to drop Dance Club and go out for cheerleader. With all the new routines I learned at camp, I think I have a chance."

Jeannie didn't think that cheerleading was a worthwhile way to spend time. Then again, one of the qualities that Jeannie liked most about Lisabeth was that she sometimes did allow herself to be swept away by things that were not serious or worthwhile.

Listening as Lisabeth explained the fine art of cheerleading, Jeannie walked on. Even if she was frivolous enough to want to try out, she knew she would be rejected because of her height. She was full-grown at five-foot nine. She had even filled out, put some meat on her scarecrow frame, but cheerleaders were always little and cute like Lisabeth Richman.

Because the girls were early, they lingered on the wide front steps and watched other students filing in. Jeannie, paying less and less attention to Lisabeth, examined faces —familiar and unfamiliar—in the crowd. One attracted her particular attention. A boy with curly blond hair. He was thin. He walked with a crutch and an odd, rocking gait.

It was Kit. He had spotted her, too. She knew that by the uncomfortable way he jerked his head to one side when she tried to catch his eye.

Despite her promises, she had hardly seen him during the last year. As he had predicted, she'd been as faithless as Old-Death-and-Dying. Getting together with him had not worked. He would not come to her house, nor did he want her at his. She could have tried to work this out, but she never did.

A few times, they met in a drugstore down the street from where he lived. Jeannie hadn't liked that. She was afraid of encountering Eleanor, who was a junior at Jackson—a prom queen, a cheerleader. Jeannie and Kit never ran into each other at Hanover, either, because his therapy was during the week and she only worked on Saturdays.

It had never occurred to her that he would be at Jackson this year. Seeing him on the steps, Jeannie knew he was angry, that he did not want to talk with her. To deal with her guilty feelings and carry out her intention of being more outgoing at school, Jeannie grabbed Lisabeth by the arm.

"Come on," she urged, pulling her friend through the crowd toward Kit. "I want you to meet someone." She also wanted Lisabeth at her side for support.

"Kit," she called, rushing to catch up to him. He moved quickly, trying to escape from her, but by the time he reached the front hall, she was there, too. Then she planted herself right in front of him, forcing him to stop.

"Lisabeth Richman," she said breathlessly, "this is Kit Hayden."

"Hello, Kit," Lisabeth said, pulling off her glasses and looking up at him in a misty, myopic way. Without glasses, Lisabeth was helpless, and Jeannie had never seen her whip them off like that.

If Jeannie had mentioned Kit to Lisabeth, her friend didn't seem to remember. Kit wasn't a topic for discussion with Jeannie.

"Hello," Kit answered begrudgingly. He didn't look at Jeannie but at some indeterminate spot behind her left shoulder.

"What's the matter?" Lisabeth asked, gesturing at his crutch and making an out-of-season joke. "Ski accident?"

"No," Kit replied without hesitation. "I was wounded in a duel."

As Lisabeth laughed, Jeannie looked down, realizing that as Kit only used one crutch now, he had only one brace. All that was visible were the metal clamps on the side of his shoe. Polio hadn't occurred to Lisabeth. In a year, everyone had forgotten about polio.

Shifting her gaze, Jeannie saw that Kit was anxious to get away from them. She wanted to detain him. She meant to be helpful, yet because she was uneasy, what she said was not particularly helpful. "What happened to the other crutch?"

Kit frowned. "Sent it back to the March of Dimes," he replied, with a familiar knife-edge tone to his voice. "Thought some other one-legged crip could use it. But look at you, Jeannie West, you look different, too. You look like a peppermint candy wrapped in cellophane."

The laugh that rose from her throat was anything but

5 4

spontaneous. Kit was making fun of the white Shetland sweater and red-and-white plaid kilt she'd chosen so carefully for the first day back at school. She was irritated at him and not going to let him humiliate her in front of Lisabeth.

"Well, you," she said, rummaging through her head for the right words, "look like a hunter who can't tell the difference between a duck and his own hat."

Lisabeth, sucking on the earpiece to her glasses, listened wide-eyed to her friend fencing with this strange, unfriendly boy.

Jeannie poked her. "Come on, we'd better get to homeroom." She had made her effort. It had been a failure, and she wasn't going to let Kit spoil the beginning of her sophomore year.

As she and Lisabeth headed off, she offered a brief explanation. "I knew him when he was in the hospital. He had polio."

Lisabeth put her glasses back on. "He'd be kind of cute if he smiled."

Jeannie blinked. It had never occurred to her that Kit was or wasn't cute. As she struggled to keep herself from asking Lisabeth how—without glasses on—she had been able to determine *what* Kit looked like, she heard the noise behind them.

Even in a crowded and noisy hallway, she recognized the sound of a body falling to the floor. The thud was followed immediately by a collective moan from the milling students. She spun around. There on the floor, facing away from her, was Kit. Arms and hands were reaching down to help.

"Leave me alone. Back off," he shouted. "I don't need help, dammit. Back off, I said." He didn't need help. In only a few seconds, he was back on his feet, crutch under his left arm, marching lopsidedly away.

All day, Jeannie couldn't shake that picture from her head. She assumed she had been responsible for starting him off at Jackson in such a miserable manner. She never had a chance to apologize, though, because they weren't in any of the same classes. Jeannie didn't know if he was entering as a freshman or as a sophomore, if his tutoring had been successful enough that he didn't have to stay back a year.

At three o'clock, when classes were over, she and Lisabeth headed for the *Banner* room. The first person the girls ran into was a big, hulking junior named Mike O'Connor. He was sports editor. He was also a football player. Usually, Jeannie was shy in his presence, but today she forced herself to approach him. Sophomores did sports reporting and did not write hard news or contribute to the literary page, since these areas were traditionally reserved for juniors and seniors. Although she wasn't particularly interested in sports, she wanted to see if Mike would let her do features for his section.

Before she could ask him, however, he called out to her. "Hey, come have a look. Over here. Someone has pinned the craziest thing up on the bulletin board."

Jeannie's heart bounced rubber balls against her chest wall. She knew what she was about to see. The handwriting was less precise. It was in black pen instead of pencil, but the signature was the same. After a year's absence, Yeti was back.

alone, always alone, i cried, even more alone in a sea of three thousand indifferent faces, being rocked mercilessly, dreaming of belonging but never belonging, always different, feeling the sea's cruelty turn lips blue and legs numb, knowing it makes me cruel, too. fear breaks over the rocks, fear of sharks and of drowning darkness, and a fear of falling, falling, falling to black depths with no way to struggle up for air.

YETI

"Yeti? Who is Yeti?" Mike questioned, as she and Lisabeth read the message. "And what does it mean? Why on our bulletin board? Who put it there?"

Jeannie knew who Yeti was and what the message meant. She knew who had put it there and that it was meant for her. Like it or not, Kit was back in her life. He was not someone she could ignore. She felt somehow responsible for his well-being. And at that moment, she found herself wishing that she did not have a conscience. What she wanted more than anything was to be as carefree as Lisabeth.

"Wow! That sure is weird," Lisabeth agreed as she twirled her glasses in one hand and looked at Mike O'Connor.

That opinion was immediately contradicted by another voice. Anna Dorado, the sharp-faced senior who edited the paper, unpinned the message from the board. "I think you're wrong. I think it's one of the most sensitive, gutsy pieces of writing I've seen around here. And, whoever Yeti is, I'm going to print it on the literary page of the first issue."

Jeannie smiled. She admired Anna's decisiveness and wondered, at the same time, what Kit was going to think when his writing appeared in the *Banner*.

Her thoughts were interrupted by Mike's rumbling voice. He grinned at her. "Jeannie," he said, shuffling his feet as he talked, "you look swell in that outfit, and, well . . . I'm glad you're here because I need help covering football. Do you know anything about football?"

She didn't. She did know that it was unusual to find

herself looking *up* at a boy. Kit and Yeti vanished from her head as she answered Mike's question with one of her own.

"When do I start?" she asked, straightening her shoulders and grinning back at him.

7

$\mathcal{J}$EANNIE whirled into the kitchen with the force of an autumn hurricane. "Morning, morning, morning," she said, by way of greeting to her mother, her father, and Jill. "Can I help? Oh, gosh, I'm late, and you're waiting. I'm sorry."

Weekdays, everyone in the West household was too busy to spend a leisurely breakfast together, so Saturday morning was set aside as Pancake Time. This particular October Saturday, Jeannie didn't have time to participate in the ritual.

Today was the opening game of the Jackson high football season and the day of her first writing assignment for the *Banner*. Mike O'Connor had asked her to do an interview on people's thoughts about the coming season. Though excited, she had not taken time to figure out how football had become as important to her as biology and English.

Jill examined her sister with an eleven-year-old's intensity. "Since when has Jeannie gotten so interested in clothes? She has a new sweater on, Mom. Can I get a new sweater?"

Jeannie considered giving her sister a good shake, but she didn't. Controlling herself, she slid into her place without comment.

Her mother, sensing trouble, put two pancakes on Jeannie's plate and smiled at her across the table. "You look especially nice today—doesn't she, Tom?"

Jeannie's father winked. "Pretty is as pretty does," he said.

Lowering her head, Jeannie cut into the unbuttered pancakes. She had tried hard to look good, but it had never occurred to her as she dressed in the blue plaid Bermuda shorts, white shirt, and backward-buttoned yellow sweater that anyone in her family would notice. When she pulled on the yellow knee socks and slipped into her penny loafers, she forgot that Jill, always observant, was rapidly approaching her teens. Now her sister was examining everything—from her feet to the blue headband that tucked her hair behind her ears.

Jeannie dropped her fork. She wanted to leave before Jill said something provocative enough to start an argument. After draining the rest of her milk, she jumped to her feet. "Sorry, but I've got to run. I'm due over at the field, and I shouldn't be late."

Before she ran out, she was careful to get her notebook and pen and give each of her parents a kiss on the cheek. Her exit wasn't quite swift enough to miss hearing a few parting observations from the breakfast nook.

"Oh, Tom, she's growing up. She really is," her mother said quietly.

Jill was much louder. "I think it's disgusting," she commented.

Disgusting or not, Jeannie was full of anticipation as she rode the bus to school. For once, she didn't care that she did not have Lisabeth's protective company. Lisabeth had made the cheerleading squad. This morning she would be with them—with Kit's sister, too—practicing their routines.

Jeannie was on her own, but she did not feel lonely. The pen and notebook gave her a reason for being at the game. She had learned to deal with all kinds of people at Hanover. Now she thought it was time to bring that confidence to school.

As she threaded her way through the early arrivals at the football field, however, her sense of confidence began to seep away. She was again tall, gawky Jeannie West, visible in any crowd but today even more visible because of the way she had chosen to dress. Pulling off the headband, she stuffed it in her pocket.

Everywhere she looked there were people—parents, students, little children—yet she wasn't sure how to begin. The team ran onto the field for warm-up exercises, and the assembling crowd clapped with enthusiasm. With shoulder pads and helmets, the players looked huge, unfamiliar. She didn't recognize anybody. Turning from them, she surveyed the bleachers. Suddenly she missed Lisabeth and was angry at her friend for deserting her.

At that moment, someone tapped her shoulder. "Getting good stuff?" a voice rumbled.

Wheeling around, Jeannie looked up. It took her several seconds to realize that the chunky player standing before her was Mike O'Connor. "Mmm . . . oh, hi. Yeah, sure."

Mike loosened the chin strap on his helmet. "Wearing the old school colors, too. Nice."

Jeannie's face was hot. The still-blank notebook slipped from her hand. Mike bent down and grabbed it. As he held it out to her, she saw that he was, at the same time, offering her a giant yellow chrysanthemum. People wore them on football-game days to show they were rooting for Jackson.

She was overwhelmed. Mike O'Connor, a junior, a

football player, was presenting her with a chrysanthe-mum.

"Swell . . . I mean, thanks, Mike. Listen, I'm going to try and do a good article. And the flower—well, thanks again."

Mike's expression, because of the helmet and black crescents of grease smeared under his eyes, was hard to read, but his grin indicated he found her flustered state charming. "Hmm . . . yeah, I found the flower on the ground. Someone must have lost it. Doesn't have a pin or anything. Sorry."

Jeannie didn't care. Knowing Mike hadn't gone out and bought the flower for her relieved some of her ner-vousness. "Well," she said, smiling up at him and wishing she knew something about football. "I hope it's a good game. I hope you play well."

Mike looked as if she had wedged a slice of lemon be-tween his teeth. "I'm only second-string," he grimaced. "I probably won't get to play."

"Maybe you will," she said encouragingly. "Maybe someone will be sick or something."

Mike began to back up. "I like your attitude. You're a nice kid, J.W. And kind of pretty, too."

But Jeannie had no time to revel in these words be-cause he had hardly gotten them out when a low-flying seagull deposited a big glob of black-and-white droppings on the top of his helmet. When Mike realized what had happened, he cringed.

"Don't worry," she told him, swallowing her laughter. "Maybe that was just the bluebird of happiness dropping a little luck on your head."

As she was waving him back onto the field, she was aware, belatedly, that someone, not too far away, had been snapping pictures of them. It was Kit.

She had hardly seen him in the three weeks since school had begun. The Yeti message had been printed in the *Banner*, stirring up curiosity among the students, but no one seemed to know who had written it.

"Kit," she called. He was retreating, digging his crutch into the dirt at the side of the field. "Kit—wait up. Please."

To her surprise, he stopped. Jeannie rushed forward to join him. "Hey, were you just taking pictures of me with Mike?"

Kit shook his head. "Not of you. Of O'Connor with the bird guano oozing down his helmet."

Jeannie examined the camera hung around his neck. "I didn't know you took pictures."

"I didn't. Not before the polio. Started last year. If I can't play football, I've got to do something. So I'm taking pictures."

"But you never *played* football!"

"Same difference," he said. "If I can't go to Yosemite and climb Half Dome, I take and develop pictures. If I feel like it, I even let Anna Dorado publish them in the *Banner*."

"Just pictures?" she asked, twirling the chrysanthemum in her fingers. "Why don't you join the staff and write?"

"Not me," he said curtly. "I don't write. I leave that to you. When you're not being Dr. Jeannie West, you can be Jeannie West, girl poet, or Jeannie West, girl reporter."

Jeannie looked down at her blank-paged notebook. "Hey, Kit," she said impulsively, "I am supposed to be reporting today. But I don't understand football. Could you . . . would you explain a few things?"

His hasty laugh was harsh and uncompromising.

"Why? So you can impress O'Connor? You really are a wonk. My sister and your buddy Lisabeth, too. Look at them out there, will you?"

Turning, Jeannie looked. The cheerleading squad, dressed in trim blue-and-yellow outfits, was chanting and moving in unison.

> *Go back, go back, go back to the woods,*
> *'Cause you haven't, you haven't, you haven't*
>   *Got the goods.*
> *And you haven't got the rhythm and you haven't*
>   *Got the jazz,*
> *And you haven't got the team that Jackson High*
>   *has!*

"They look like bluejays hopping on hot cement," Kit scoffed.

Jeannie liked his simile, but she was not about to admit it. She shrugged. "I think they look like dragonflies floating on the wind." Then, without waiting for his reaction, she turned and strode away.

It had been a confident gesture, but it didn't make the rest of the day better. Jeannie never did any interviewing. She sat by herself at one end of the bleachers watching the incomprehensible game. When she saw Lisabeth joking with the rest of the cheerleading squad, she glowered.

After a while, she began to wish that she had been nicer to Kit. Being with him would have been better than the humiliation of being alone.

Jackson lost the game 24 to 9. The scoreboard said so. Just when she planned to flee for the comfort of her home, someone jostled her elbow. The notebook fell from her hand, slid through the slats of the bleachers, and dropped to the ground far below.

She could have left it there, but because she had not done anything right the whole day, she forced herself to climb down and make her way underneath the bleachers to retrieve the notebook. It was a dim and smelly place. The ground was littered with soft-drink bottles, candy wrappers, and orange peels. A scruffy-looking dog was devouring a chunk of pink caramel corn.

As she picked her way through the mess, she regretted her decision. Still, she would not allow herself to turn back. Trying to ignore the occasional dripping of scummy unidentified substances, she searched until she found her pad, grimy but otherwise all right.

Anxious to escape from under the creaking wooden structure, she turned around. It was then that she saw Kit. He was sitting on a metal support pole at the edge of the stands, leaning his chin on his crutch and staring at her.

"You followed me," she said accusingly.

He nodded.

"Why?"

Patting the pole, he gestured for her to sit next to him. Without taking time to examine her intentions or his, she did.

"I followed you," he began, "because I was a louse before. And because you didn't look as if you were having a very good time today."

"I wasn't," she answered, surprised to find that after a year's lapse she could still expose some of her feelings in front of Kit. Somehow the dim light behind the bleachers made it easier for her to speak unselfconsciously.

"I wasn't, either," he told her.

"Don't you have friends to be with?" she asked, beginning to pull thin petals from the chrysanthemum.

"Don't you?" As soon as these words were out of his mouth, Kit looked as though he regretted the abruptness with which he had answered. "Look, the guys I knew before—they're doing other things. There's too much stinking pity over what they can do and I can't. Except—Dmitri. He doesn't always think of me as a cripple. He even thinks we can try some easy rock climbing . . ."

Jeannie was listening, yet she wasn't. There was something else, something important, she wanted to ask. "Kit?"

"What?"

"Do you think you and I could try again to be friends?"

He didn't answer immediately. Instead he began drawing patterns in the dirt with the tip of his crutch. "Maybe," he agreed.

Encouraged, Jeannie continued. "I've changed some. Grown up, I think." When she paused, she remembered Mike O'Connor's compliment. "I have changed, haven't I? Do you think I'm prettier?"

Kit squinted as if he were trying to see her better in the half-light. "You're okay," he said.

"Just okay?"

"Look, Jeannie, I live with Eleanor, who is obsessed by her beauty, and I find it a boring topic." Then he changed the subject. "Tell me about your story. Did you get what you needed for your article?"

Jeannie shook her head. "No, not really," she said, yet as she spoke she suddenly began to realize that she *did* have something to write. Not interviews, not quite a story either, but a piece with words that flowed. She was going to write about what she had seen and felt that day—about dressing up, about being alone, about cheerleaders and about a yellow chrysanthemum, about searching for a notebook under dark bleachers. If Yeti could write about personal thoughts, she could, too. Jumping lightly to her feet, she poised there, swaying from side to side.

"You look," Kit said, putting his hands up and starting to edge inch by inch along a metal pole above his head, "like a ballerina about to dance the solo in *Swan Lake*."

"And you," she said, as she watched him move along, using the strength in his hands and arms, "look like a climber working his way up Half Dome."

A shadow crossed Kit's face, and Jeannie was distressed that she had mentioned Half Dome. Then, recovering, Kit sent a smile in her direction. "I will climb it. Not yet. But someday. And meanwhile, I like your suggestion. Let's try being friends."

8

ℬY ALLOWING a stream of thoughts and words to flow out on paper, Jeannie wrote her piece. It seemed better than an ordinary newspaper story, yet she was dissatisfied. Although the piece was somewhat poetic, it was not *her* kind of poetry.

After Mike and Anna agreed to print it, Mike remarked that one Yeti was enough for any school. "Next time, J.W.," he said, "keep your work more upbeat, if you can."

Knowing he was right, Jeannie didn't protest. On Thursday, when her story was published, another note from Yeti appeared in the *Banner* room. Reading it, Jeannie saw again how inadequate her own try had been.

> in the dimness of twilight, fear is unpeeled, leaving people naked, with no sense of ordinary shame, so they can say what they truly mean when they have shed the layers of pretense they wear in their everyday lives. unselfconsciously they can talk, making plans and promises, letting hearts unclench in expectation. in sheltering darkness all things seem possible and shoots of joy stretch up, reaching for sunlight. yet in the harsh light of morning, regret blows like the northwest wind and promises made are like half-eaten apples rotting on the ground as

people reach for capes of leaves to protect their
bared hearts.

YETI

That night Jeannie called Kit. Despite the discomfort involved, she wanted to reach him. The first time she dialed the number, Eleanor picked up the phone and Jeannie, unnerved, hung up. A little later when she tried, his mother answered. Jeannie wanted to hang up again when the woman's tiger-purr voice asked who was calling and what was wanted with Kit. But she didn't.

Instead, she mumbled that she needed to talk to Kit about work for the *Banner*. When Kit picked up the extension and said hello, the receiver Mrs. Hayden was holding did not click back into place.

"Kit, this is Jeannie," she began, feeling awkward and wishing his mother weren't listening in.

"What do you want?"

"Well . . ." Jeannie said.

"Mother, come on—put down the phone! This isn't your call!"

A second later the phone line lost its hollow echo. Then Jeannie managed to ask if he would come to her house for Saturday breakfast and, afterward, go to the hospital to work with her in the ward. Though there was no particular enthusiasm in his voice when he agreed, she considered a "yes" from him a significant victory.

On Saturday, she was up early helping her mother prepare pancakes and bacon. Neither of her parents was making a fuss because she had invited a boy for breakfast. Jill, on the other hand, did not show the same restraint.

"Here we go," she moaned, rolling her eyes. "Every time Jeannie falls in love, we're going to have to play show-and-tell and see if some guy thinks we're okay."

Jeannie couldn't silence her, yet when Kit came, Jill suddenly lost her voice. Jeannie didn't know whether it was the effect of seeing the brace attached to one shoe, of the crutch, or of Kit's manner.

The boy who arrived at the West doorstep at precisely 8:30 and introduced himself politely to her family did not seem to be the Kit Hayden she knew. He was dressed in neat corduroy pants and a baggy tweed jacket. He was uncharacteristically pleasant, and if he was uneasy he didn't show it.

"What class are you in, Kit?" Jeannie's father asked when they were seated in the breakfast nook.

"Sophomore, sir," Kit answered, leaning his crutch against the wall behind him. "I did home study with a tutor all last year so I wouldn't fall behind."

"Kit's taking pictures for the *Banner*," Jeannie volunteered, aware she was being overly enthusiastic. "Developing them himself, too."

Kit frowned as he piled his plate with pancakes. "Just a way to spend time," he said. "Something other people thought would be a good hobby for a post-polio patient. But I'm only doing it until I can take up climbing again."

"Climbing?" Jeannie's mother asked, as though she was sure that this boy could accomplish whatever he wanted.

"Yes," Kit answered, shifting his eyes from Dr. West to Mrs. West. "Rock climbing. Mountain climbing. I can't do it yet. They've still got me picking up marbles with my toes, lifting weights, swimming. Right now, my left leg is shorter than my right. But next Christmas, if I've grown enough—not this Christmas, but a year from now —they'll operate. After that, I should be able to climb."

Kit was sitting there discussing with her parents things she had never asked him and that he had never offered. Listening to this relaxed stranger made her wonder what had happened to the sullen boy who took such delight in being rude.

Her father managed to produce an answer to that question. "I imagine," he said between sips of coffee, "that you've spent a lot of time with adults in the last year or so."

Kit nodded.

"Does being back at school seem strange?" Her father was inquiring about something personal, but his low-key approach produced an immediate answer from Kit.

"Yes, it does. It might be easier, though, if team sports weren't more important at Jackson—more important to some people, that is—than schoolwork."

Jeannie felt as though she were a kite floating in the air. She wished someone would tug at that string and let her back into the conversation. When she sneaked a sideways glance at Jill, she discovered that her sister was staring up at Kit with open-mouthed awe.

"You seem to take your work very seriously," Jeannie's mother said, passing the platter to Kit for a second time.

"I do."

"A little learning, they say, is a dangerous thing," Dr. West commented.

Kit smiled. "And a lot of learning is even more dangerous?"

"Probably so," her father declared, smiling back. "But worth it."

"Yes, sir. I think so. That's why I'm planning on college. I might like teaching, I think—working with kids. As long as I can climb, too . . ."

Though Jeannie's parents were finding out things about Kit, they didn't know about Yeti. Nor had they seen the shrunken left leg, which was going to prevent Kit from realizing his dreams about climbing. He might know to address her father as "sir," and display friendly adult manners, but underneath he wasn't that different from the angry boy she had known at Hanover.

She was aware of his anger as they entered the hospital and followed the pink footprints to Pediatrics. "I'm not very happy about this," he told her, his jaw held so rigidly he hardly moved it as he spoke.

"About what?"

"Being back here. Going into the ward."

"But, Kit," she protested, "you come here every week for therapy."

"Yeah, but that's marbles—not going back and looking at the place where I *lived*."

Jeannie nodded. Kit was tense, but she thought she knew how to deal with him. "You don't have to come with me. Go home if you want. I'll understand."

"Oh, you're very understanding when you want to be, Jeannie with the light-brown hair."

She stopped at the O.T. room to pick up her apron. "Hey," she pleaded. "Didn't we decide to stop all this arguing and be friends?"

Kit sighed. "Yes—right. It's just that this place makes me feel like the sick, wonky kid I was a year ago."

"I'm sorry."

"So why are you sorry? Why are you *always* apologizing?"

Jeannie glared. He was impossible, really impossible. Instead of squabbling with him, she could have been at a Jackson High football game, watching Mike and Lisabeth.

"Stop picking on me," she said. Then, without waiting to see what he would say or do, she strode into the ward and began moving from bed to bed greeting all the children.

After a few minutes, Kit came in. Without saying much, he started walking along the aisles. From the pockets of his baggy jacket, he produced coins, balloons, disappearing scarves—everything but a live rabbit. During his year at home, Kit seemed to have developed into an amateur magician.

Jeannie stared after him. Every time she was so fed up that she wanted him out of her life forever, he managed to do something surprising enough to make her forgive him.

A girl with coloring books and checkers was of no particular interest compared to a boy with a crutch who could make coins appear from behind an ear or roses pop out of an empty hand. The crutch was like a special kind of magic wand, proof to the sick children that Kit was one of them.

When Alonzo came by with a pail, Kit talked football with the older man and did a card trick. For Cabot, he produced more roses. Watching, Jeannie was aware that she wanted to write about the two Kits that she knew, but she was sure no story of hers would capture the complexity she was seeing.

She noticed that Kit showed particular sensitivity with the burn patients. Because they tended to be in a lot of pain, they were often angry and petulant. As Kit limped along among them, pulling out new tricks, twisting long, thin balloons into the shapes of animals, no one complained, no one cried.

When Martin Storey showed up on Saturday morning rounds, he was delighted to find Kit entertaining the ward.

"I must say, I am impressed," he said when Kit came from the corner where the respirator patients had been watching him in their overhead mirrors.

"Don't be," Kit said with a shrug. "It's all done by cheating. And, besides, it's a hobby for a polio—just something to do until I can start climbing."

Martin frowned at this answer. "Kit, my friend—Christopher . . ."

Kit laughed. "You're sounding just like Dr. Goldberger."

Martin Storey nodded. "Perhaps, but I see you in there with those children and I marvel at your sleight of hand. Yet, when I compliment you, you cheapen your skill by calling it therapy for the handicapped."

Jeannie watched Kit's mouth begin to pull taut like a clothesline. "I'm sick and tired of being congratulated for things that don't count—stinking sick and tired of being pitied because of my limp and this crutch. I can't wait for surgery. I can't wait to get back to rock climbing."

"Kit," Martin said, "I don't mean to be a killjoy, don't mean to clip your wings, but you are not destined to be a climber. Not with that leg. You must face up to—"

"But I will climb, Doctor. You told me to struggle to get well, and I am doing that in the best way I can. So stop slapping me down.

"And while you're at it," he continued, furious but keeping his voice controlled so that the young patients could not hear him, "I'm also sick of this business of wings and roots. You are clipping my wings when you dare tell me—tell me when I'm not sixteen yet—that I'll *never* climb. I'll pick up frigging marbles like a performing monkey if it makes me strong enough to climb."

When Kit was finished with Jeannie's uncle, he turned to her. "I'm leaving. If you want to come, it's okay. If you want to stick around, that's okay by me, too." Then he hobbled off down the hall.

After Jeannie paused to offer her uncle a quick, apologetic look, she fled toward the elevator, trying to catch up with Kit.

"Oh, Kit," she moaned. "How can you ruin such a wonderful morning this way? You're so terrific with the

74

children, and then this. What happens to you? Why do you act this way?"

He made no attempt to answer her questions, but by the time they were coming out of the hospital, he looked somewhat less fierce.

"My folks and Jill—they liked you a lot," Jeannie said, determined that she and Kit would not talk about climbing. "You passed with them. You really did."

Kit stuck out his crutch and stopped her. As they stood on the sidewalk together, she realized for the first time how much he had grown in the last year. He was as tall as she was now. His blue eyes were level with her brown ones. "What about you, Jeannie? Do I pass with you? Why do you make me feel like a little boy whose teacher is picking on him?"

Jeannie brushed a stray lock of hair back behind her ear. "Yes . . . you pass with me," she told him hesitantly, "sometimes. When you're not making *me* feel like an innocent pupil taking a spanking for something I didn't do."

"That's not a very good simile."

Jeannie smiled wanly. "Maybe it's not."

Kit examined her face in silence for a moment. "Jeannie?"

"What?"

"Will you come climbing with me next weekend? Easy stuff. With Dmitri."

Jeannie wanted to scream at him. Climbing. He was always thinking about climbing, even right after her uncle had told him he would never be a climber again. "Oh, Kit . . . Kit—"

"Don't lecture, Jeannie. I asked you a simple question. Will you climb with me next weekend? Yes or no."

Jeannie took a deep breath. "Yes," she answered softly. "Okay, I will."

Kit tucked his crutch back under his left arm. Then he leaned forward and pulled a string of iridescent scarves from the pocket of her yellow apron. She had passed, too. And she was not altogether thrilled about it.

9

BY THE following Sunday, Kit's proposed climb with Jeannie had become a full-scale expedition. Since Kit was bringing his friend Dmitri Beals, he suggested that Jeannie ask Anna, Mike O'Connor, and Lisabeth.

Lisabeth, Mike, and Anna were all enthusiastic. To them rock climbing sounded like an unusual and exciting way to spend an afternoon. Anna wanted to do a newspaper story with Kit supplying the pictures. Lisabeth, who was getting contact lenses that week, was interested because of Dmitri, whom she found incredibly handsome. With Mike, it seemed to be a question of challenge. Anything a boy with a crutch and a brace could do, he should be able to manage.

On Sunday morning, Mike picked them up in his father's car. Then they headed for Twin Peaks, where Dmitri knew of a good climb.

In the car, Lisabeth and Mike did most of the talking. They discussed what they had brought for lunch, football, the Winter Prom, and whether white ankle socks looked better up or rolled down. Jeannie tried to talk with them, but Anna said little. Anna usually didn't speak unless she had something to say. Dmitri didn't seem to be much of a talker, either.

Kit was absolutely silent. Jeannie didn't know if he was thinking about the climb, feeling frightened, or sorry he had suggested the whole thing. When they reached their

77

destination, however, his manner changed. Suddenly he was communicative. Gesturing, he began to explain about the rock and the skills necessary to climb it.

"It's not a race or a competition," he said. "We're just going to start at the bottom and make it to the top slowly —step by step—carefully. And don't be scared. No one's going to get hurt."

Listening to the reassuring tone of his voice, Jeannie noticed that this was the same way he spoke to the children in the hospital. While he spoke, he used his crutch as though it were a teacher's pointer instead of something to support a crippled leg.

When Jeannie first looked at the rock face, it didn't seem very high. It was steep at the bottom, but the upper half was a succession of gray-green rocky ledges. She had scaled cliffs near Sutro Baths with her father and Uncle Martin, cliffs that were as steep as those before her. Still, she had never been thrilled with the idea of heights.

She was not the only hesitant one. Lisabeth, her eyes watering from the unaccustomed lenses, threw herself down on a patch of dried grass at the base of the rock and began to laugh. "You guys must think I'm crazy. I can't go up *that*. I'd fall and break something."

"The bottom part seems tricky," Mike said. "You sure we don't need a rope?"

"I don't think so," Dmitri said. "It's not as hard as it looks."

Anna seemed to be encouraged by Dmitri's words. "I'm going to try it, but I'd like to follow someone— watch what someone is doing."

Anna made Jeannie feel less fearful. She was bigger, stronger, and more agile than Anna Dorado. If climbing this cliff was acceptable to a sensible senior like her, it was all right for Jeannie.

Kit didn't appear to be worrying. "You must always

think about *three*," he told them. "Have three secure points before you move. Never move a hand unless the other one and both feet are secure. Never a foot unless you have two good handholds and one foot stable. And think about balance.

"Don't look back. Lean out just enough that you can see your feet, enough that your weight presses your feet *into* the rock. Concentrate on what you're doing. And, Lisabeth, you can do it. It's hardly more than a scramble."

Lisabeth laughed, but she made no move to pick herself up from the grass. She had already decided to stay below. Watching Dmitri climb, Jeannie decided, would probably keep Lisabeth occupied for the day.

"Now," Kit continued, after consulting with Dmitri. "Dmitri is going to demonstrate some moves. So come over here, and we'll practice traversing—going sideways —before we go up the rock."

Mike was standing behind Jeannie when Dmitri began to crawl crablike across the lower portion of the wall. "You really going to do this, J.W.?" he asked.

As she nodded, she was aware for the first time that she didn't particularly like being called by her initials.

"Well, the top doesn't look too tough," he conceded. "Seems okay, I guess."

Jeannie was surprised to see that Mike suffered from the same kinds of uncertainties that she did. But if she and Anna were going up the cliff, he had to go, too.

Watching Dmitri, Jeannie forgot about Mike. Dmitri negotiated the rock, climbing across and back near the ground as if he were doing a ballet with the rock as his stage. Nothing Kit had told her prepared her for the fact that rock climbing had such grace to it. Dmitri's movements were both flowing and precise. He was careful, surefooted. He made climbing look easy.

As Jeannie stood there fascinated, she realized that

words were shifting about inside her head. Words that described what she was seeing yet didn't make complete sense. She didn't know what to do with them or where they belonged. She had no pencil with which to write them down. Nor was she sure that what she'd write would make sense.

Her trancelike state was broken by a gasp from Lisabeth. "Oh, Dmitri," she called out appreciatively. "That's terrific. But too hard for me. I'm scared."

Jeannie wasn't. She knew now that she was going to touch the rock and dance across it slowly as Dmitri was doing. The half-articulated words inside her head had cooled her fear. Kit was not being wild and reckless. She was about to do something beautiful. She was glad to be there.

Leaning on his crutch, Kit made sure that Jeannie, Anna, and Mike each got a chance to get a feel for the rock. Keeping them a few feet off the ground, he gave advice as Dmitri demonstrated techniques for handholds and footholds.

After an hour of this preparation, Dmitri and Kit decided they were ready. Then Dmitri started climbing up. Anna was to follow him, then Mike, then Jeannie, then Kit. Each was to copy Dmitri's route to the top.

She watched as each of the three ahead of her started out. Kit was spacing them carefully, so she stood there for a long time before he told her that she, too, could begin. Without any hesitation, she took hold of the rock.

Climbing, she quickly discovered, was not as easy as Dmitri had made it look. Going up did not feel as safe as moving sideways. She was only eight or ten feet off the ground when she began to tremble in a way she could not control. From below, she could hear Kit calling to her.

"Relax. You're pressing too hard. Ease up. Go slowly. Even more slowly. If you ease up, your muscles will relax.

Now reach for that bucket—that big handhold—up beyond your right hand. Good. Yes."

Grateful for his concern, she did as he said. When she got to a spot where both her feet were on a small outcropping, Kit encouraged her to stand there, to breathe regularly, to rest. Kit, she realized, had to pull himself up this same rock.

She peered down from her ledge. He had discarded his crutch and was beginning to edge his way up the rock. His movements were not beautiful or fluid like Dmitri's. Yet, with arms and one leg strong from a year and a half of physical therapy, he *was* climbing.

When he saw her watching, he was annoyed. "Don't look back," he barked. "Take care of yourself, not me."

Knowing he was right, Jeannie concentrated on her own climbing. It was exhausting. Her legs were strong from dancing, but her arms ached from unaccustomed exertion. She inched along, hoping her strength wouldn't give out.

A quick check told her that Dmitri, Anna, and Mike had made it. Well, she would, too. Ignoring skinned knuckles and a scraped knee, she managed to scale the last few feet of sheer rock. Then she moved quickly up the sloping ledges to the top. There Dmitri shook her hand.

"You did well," he said.

"Thanks," she replied, dropping into a heap beside Anna. She had done it.

Then, peering over the edge, she saw Kit approaching. Despite the way his left leg kept buckling, he was doing what her uncle had said he would never do again. This was not Yosemite or Half Dome. It was only a climb of sixty feet or so. When she had been on the rock, it had seemed like a mountain. To Kit still struggling there, she figured, it also seemed a long way.

A few minutes later, it was over. Kit had pulled himself

on top with the others. They were all together looking out on a spectacular view of San Francisco and the Bay. Below, Lisabeth was waving as she went through one of her cheerleading routines. Jeannie, feeling a sense of exhilaration, waved back.

"Well . . ." Kit said, trying to mask the fact that he was breathing hard. "Now there's the little matter of getting down."

Jeannie had never thought about getting down, and she knew she hadn't saved enough energy for that. Kit had led her into something crazy. "Oh, Kit!"

"Whoa, slow down. Wait—there's a back route—a trail, over there, which some of you may want to take. Do you mind, Jeannie?"

He was teasing, she realized then. He knew they'd use the trail.

"That's how I'm going," Anna said. "What do we do? Just follow that steep little path?"

Kit nodded. "Yes—right, you three then. Dmitri?"

"I'm climbing."

"Me, too," Kit declared.

"But, Kit," Jeannie protested, worrying that he shouldn't risk it.

His eyes bored into her like a high-speed drill. He looked as if he might kill her if she suggested he was handicapped by his leg.

"I've got to go back down the rock," he said flatly. "I can't balance or walk without the crutch."

Anger welled up inside her. This was the first moment all day that she wished they were alone. Then she could reason with him. In front of the others, he would not tolerate her concern.

She gritted her teeth as she, Mike, and Anna headed for the trail. Walking down, she quickly discovered, was not easy either. The backs of her legs, tired from climbing, ached with every step she took.

In about ten minutes, they arrived back at the patch of grass where Lisabeth was waiting. In the same amount of time, Dmitri had lowered himself smoothly down the rock face. Kit was not far behind.

Looking up, Jeannie watched him. He was straining for a difficult foothold. His left leg flailed in midair. Something was wrong. Frightened, she turned to Dmitri, but before any words came out, it happened.

Kit's foot missed the niche, his hands peeled loose, and he slid down the last fifteen feet of rock. At the last moment, his fingers caught the branches of a small bush, slowing his fall. When he dropped onto the grass, Dmitri was there to help.

Kit's hands were raw and beginning to bleed. He'd opened a cut on his upper lip, and the left knee of his pants was damp with blood.

"It's all right. I'm all right," Kit said over and over.

Jeannie moved forward. "Do we have first-aid supplies?"

"Sure," Dmitri said.

Kit was beckoning to her. "That's right, Jeannie. You're the doctor here. Come on. Get the stuff. Fix me up."

Kit *was* all right. Jeannie cleaned and bandaged the cuts. Kit did not complain about anything except her desire to examine his left knee. He wouldn't permit that. He did not want anyone staring at his withered left leg.

Kit's calmness wrapped itself around the others like a warm blanket. The fall, its consequences, began to seem unimportant. Unimportant to all except Jeannie.

Soon, everyone was sprawled out, eating. Kit, ignoring his injuries, was talking with great animation. He teased Jeannie, telling her she'd looked like a ballet dancer on the rock, when she should have moved like a mountain goat. He looked very happy. He was being appreciated.

Although Jeannie forced herself to join in, she wasn't able to relax. It seemed as if there were a pane of glass between herself and the others. She was disturbed that Kit had fallen, but she was also upset because she felt left out.

This was Kit's day. His party. Despite the fall—or because of it—he was a big success. Hating herself, Jeannie begrudged him that. Besides, with the others around, she and Kit could not share any easy familiarity.

If she traded similes with him, the others would laugh. The fact that Mike O'Connor watched her admiringly should have improved her mood, but it didn't. Kit, even though she had never really valued him, had seemed to be her property. Now she could see that he wasn't. He was making his own place, and she was not sure it would include her.

She still felt the same way the next morning when, taped inside the lid of her homeroom desk, she found a piece of paper with tiny writing on it.

> *though i dream of flying, dream of falling, i do not dream my own death any more, do not dream of sliding helplessly into darkness. what i do dream is myself whole, unmarked, not set apart, not suffering. laughter i dream and sunshine that rocks me gently in friendship instead of harshly in hot pain. will i ever belong in that magic circle of brilliance or will it be always only an illusion as i fly alone, fall alone?*
>
> *YETI*

Reading his words, Jeannie wanted to run through the Jackson corridors hunting him down. She needed to tell him that his message made her understand—maybe for the first time—just how much she worried about belonging, about being alone. But she didn't. It was too new a thought. It would have been too difficult to discuss.

Instead, she found Lisabeth and walked with her to first-period English. Jeannie was not ready to talk to Kit about Yeti. Between them, Yeti was still a forbidden subject.

10

$\mathcal{T}$HE CONTRAST between Yeti, who wrote messages filled with pain, and Kit Hayden, who was an active sophomore at Jackson High, continued to surprise Jeannie. Nothing, however, was more surprising than having Kit call and ask her to the Winter Ball. He had always seemed to scorn that kind of event.

Lisabeth was going with Dmitri. Jeannie wondered if her friend had arranged the dates for them both, but she didn't ask. With football season over, Lisabeth's mania about cheerleading had waned and, once again, she spent time with Jeannie. Although Jeannie still sensed distance between them, she was grateful for the other girl's company.

Without Lisabeth, Jeannie would never have selected the white satin formal. Mrs. West, who went shopping with the girls, was in favor of a long red-and-white sheath which made Jeannie feel like a candy cane. If Kit had told her she looked like a peppermint in a red plaid kilt, he was going to be equally heartless if he saw her in that dress.

The satin, which Lisabeth selected for Jeannie, was simple and different from most prom dresses. It was not floor-length. It had green velvet straps and a matching sash. The only other ornamentation was a circle of embroidered pink roses that wound around the top of the bodice. At the department store, when Jeannie looked at herself in that dress, she could not see the scarecrow—only a willowy girl who had the air of a classical ballerina.

She was excited, but once Kit had asked her, he never mentioned the event again, leaving her with qualms about the evening. She worried. She wondered whether she and Kit were going to dance. She tried to picture dancing with a partner who limped and carried a crutch.

Mid-December came quickly. Then it was the night of the dance. Lisabeth and Jeannie were at Jeannie's house helping one another get dressed. Lisabeth's dress was a long blue tulle—strapless, with little silver sequins on it. She looked, Jeannie thought, like the Dresden shepherdess that sat on the mantel in the West's living room.

When Jeannie compared herself to Lisabeth, she was dissatisfied. She was sorry that her dress did not go to the floor. Her legs looked like toothpicks beneath the satin. Her white shoes already had a smudge on one toe. She wasn't sure about the circle of pink roses, either.

She didn't want to admit her uncertainties to Lisabeth, so she kept quiet. Jill, who came in to inspect, held a running conversation with Lisabeth as the girls made their final preparation.

"I think Kit's terribly good-looking. He has this swell, distinguished look," Jill said, trying to impress Lisabeth with her maturity.

Lisabeth agreed. Still silent, Jeannie pondered these statements. She never spent any more time on Kit's looks than he spent on hers. When he wasn't around and she tried to picture him, all she could conjure up were a few blond curls and the too-close eyes.

All meditation about Kit and his looks ended as he arrived at the Wests' door with Dmitri at his side. The boys were wearing rented tuxedos and carrying corsage boxes. Opening hers, Jeannie discovered a nosegay of pink roses. She suspected Mrs. Hayden of helping to arrange for that. Left to his own devices, Kit would have given her something simpler. A single white gardenia, perhaps.

As she lifted the roses from the box, a sense of panic hit her, making her wish she did not have to go through with the evening. Kit, staring down at the roses, seemed to feel the same way. But they were trapped now by the dead-end maze of the arrangements. There would be no backing out. They'd walk to the car, where Dmitri's father was waiting to drive them. They would go to the Winter Ball.

As soon as the four arrived at Jackson and entered the suitably darkened and decorated gym, Lisabeth and Dmitri drifted off. Jeannie and Kit were left alone near the doorway, listening to the music and the sound of excited voices.

After a long moment, Kit turned to her. "Let's go up on the catwalk," he suggested. He gestured, making Jeannie realize that his camera was slung over the grip of his crutch. "I promised Anna I'd do pictures."

Jeannie agreed. She did not want to be left by herself while he went to take photographs. Together, she and Kit climbed up to the catwalk. Then, watching, they hung over the railing, looking at the activity below. A mirrored silver ball spun slowly from the ceiling, sending sprays of light in every direction. Dresses of many-colored tulle circled below them.

"From here," Kit mused, "they look like a field of flowers swaying in the wind."

Jeannie nodded. "And with the mirrors—like a field of flowers wet with dew."

Kit's smile told her he liked her comparison. "Jeannie?"

"What?"

"All that—it's going on down there without us. Do you mind?"

Slowly, Jeannie shook her head. When Kit wasn't lashing out at her, being alone with him was wonderful. In some way, however, she did care that the two of them were hidden away on a catwalk. They were at the Winter Ball, but not part of it. It bothered her that she could never simply have fun and belong.

Kit was watching her. "Jeannie?"

"What?"

"About the day we went climbing . . ."

"What about it?" she asked, gazing down at the dancers instead of across at him.

"Did you like it?"

"Parts. Some," she admitted. She had liked it before he'd fallen.

"Jeannie, when I fell—you were terrific. You didn't panic or make a fuss. I really appreciated that. And after my surgery next year, after that, I'll really be able to climb. You'll see."

Jeannie turned away. She did not want to discuss climbing. Kit would never admit that he should not climb because of his weak left leg.

"I'm going to keep on climbing no matter what you or your uncle think," Kit said challengingly.

She spun back to face him. "Oh, why, Kit? Why?" she began, aware that her words were tumbling out uncensored. "It's stupid. This whole thing you have about climbing. Why? What are you trying to *prove?*"

His voice, as he answered, was so low she had to lean closer to hear him. "I thought you understood, at least a little. But you don't, do you?" His bitter tone stung like the tip of a leather whip. "Because you gave up ballet, I should be able to give up climbing. Well, it's not that simple. To use the old hospital metaphor—if something goes bad for you, you just put down a new set of roots. Well, I am different. I have wings. I intend to use them."

Jeannie didn't want to argue with him. This discussion could ruin the whole evening. She gestured impatiently, using her purse, to which Kit's nosegay was pinned. "Why don't you take your pictures? Then we can go down and dance?"

"Dance?" Kit said, breaking out in a wild fit of laughter. "You think I can dance with a crutch and a brace?"

"If you can climb, you can dance."

Seeing his face harden, she knew she did not want to hear what he was going to say. She was unhappy with him. She was unhappy with herself. Turning, she fled across the catwalk toward the stairway which led down to the gym floor. Because of the unfamiliar high heels, she tripped. As she grabbed for the railing to break her fall, she dropped her purse.

Instead of bending to retrieve it, she righted herself and rushed on. Kit made no effort to come after her. For that she was grateful. She headed for the only sanctuary she could think of—the girls' room.

There were tears in her eyes when she ran into a large, solid obstacle. Mike O'Connor.

"Well, there you are, J.W. I've been looking for you. All over. Would you like to dance?"

Swiping at her eyes, Jeannie abandoned the idea of the girls' room. Mike wasn't a superb dancer, but he was energetic. Jeannie was graceful yet no expert at ballroom dancing, so having him as a partner was fine with her.

"My date got sick," he told her. "And I'd already rented the tux."

"I'm glad you came," Jeannie told him. A smile slid across her face as she looked up into his cheerful, freckled one.

"Why," he asked after they danced in silence for a few minutes, "were you crying before?"

She shrugged. "Feeling strange. Wondering what I was doing here."

He gave her a little squeeze. "I like you, J.W. You're sensitive. Like being nice to Kit. You're not like everyone else around here. You're kind of different. Seem to understand things. And you are pretty. Did I ever tell you that?"

Jeannie wondered if Mike could see that her feet were hardly touching the floor. When Dmitri cut in, she continued to dance on air. All Dmitri said was, "You climbed fine." He didn't have a chance to say anything else, because Mike came back and reclaimed her in a possessive way she rather liked. At intermission, he got punch for her, and they talked with some of his friends from the football team.

Jeannie had not forgotten about Kit. She wondered if he was still on the catwalk looking down. Every time she thought of him, her stomach churned nervously. And there were words swirling in her head again, words about herself and about Kit. More rivers of words she couldn't quite dam up.

Everything with Kit was difficult and intense, stirring up restless words. Mike, on the other hand, was understanding yet easy to be around. She felt as if she hadn't spent enough of the school year paying attention to him.

Being around Kit always involved suffering. Too much of this new sensation of having a head bursting with torrents of words. She did not want to spend the rest of the school year in pain.

By the time she reached these conclusions, the band was playing "Goodnight, Ladies," and Mike was holding her close. The band was drawing out the last notes of the song while they swayed in place. His lips were against her right ear. She almost thought he was kissing her, yet she never found out for certain because Kit chose that moment to come rocking forward on his crutch. He claimed her as if she were a stray dog from the pound.

"This way," he commanded, without acknowledging Mike's presence.

Mike's arms dropped away. "I guess I've got to go," she murmured apologetically. "Thanks, though. Thanks a lot!" It took great effort to thank Mike with Kit glaring at her, but she was glad she did it.

"Hurry," Kit ordered, holding out something that proved to be her purse and the now-wilted bunch of roses.

Jeannie turned from Mike and ran after Kit. He was moving too quickly for her high-heeled gait.

"Hurry up, will you?" he snapped.

Something about his angry tone reminded her of their first encounter in Hanover Hospital. "Pick up my pencil!" she said.

"What are you talking about?"

"Oh, nothing."

She wondered if Mike was watching them leave, if he would call her, if he liked her. She hoped so.

In silence, she followed Kit to the car where the others were waiting. She wasn't angry with him. She felt guilty, but not very guilty. She didn't have a single thing she wanted to say to him, so she simply kept her mouth closed.

When she and Lisabeth had let themselves in at the front door and closed it behind them, she was aware of a sense of relief. Lisabeth, as usual, was full of chatter. "Mike sure gave you a rush tonight. He's cute. Maybe even cuter than Kit. What happened with you and Kit? Where was he all night?"

Lisabeth didn't wait for answers to any of her questions, but that was fine, because Jeannie wasn't going to supply them. Lisabeth was more concerned with the fact that Dmitri had turned out to be boring.

By the time the girls said good night to Jeannie's parents, Jeannie had noticed something different about her purse. Although she guessed what it was, she didn't want to open it when Lisabeth was there.

As soon as she could manage, she left the bedroom and locked herself into the hall bathroom. Then she opened up the purse. Inside was a single sheet of notebook paper. Sitting on the edge of the tub in her white satin dress, she held the message in her hand and read it.

not deep like a cool swift river flowing downward from the continental divide, not sweet like the water made of snow melted from high peaks, but shallow like a reed-choked creek with sluggish current and placid eddies. all that lives here dies, because the creek sinks in its own sandy bed, leaving fish gasping in the shallows. shallower and shallower runs the creek until the shallow girl who would see her reflection there sees only an opaque, stagnant pool with water bugs and gasping trout. shallow, whisper the dying reeds, shallow, shallow, shallow.

YETI

For a long time, Jeannie stayed where she was, holding the paper in her hands. She wanted to cry, but no tears came. When Lisabeth tapped at the door, she did not answer. Once again, words were creating spinning storms inside her head. For the first time, she was beginning to see what she was going to have to do with those words.

She needed to pull them from her head, capture them

in her own kind of message. Not a newspaper story. Not a copy of the writing Kit produced. He—Kit—had accused her of being shallow. Well, sometimes she was, but not always.

Despite the way Kit's words hurt her, they did make her think. She didn't want to be shallow. It was time, she thought, to begin searching for the deeper parts of herself. Like an Eskimo ice-fishing, she would chop a hole in the ice, put down a line, and draw up what she found below. Her words. All the half-hidden, little-understood feelings. About herself first. Then about Kit. About Mike O'Connor, too.

Standing up, she let Kit's message float down into the wastebasket. Then, with only a small pang, she unpinned the nosegay of dead roses and let it fall in there, too. She had an idea—something she hoped she could do. Maybe. Maybe she could write a poem.

Winter 1957

11

I<small>F IT</small> hadn't been for the sound of rain beating against the windowpanes, Jeannie wouldn't have noticed the spider. Yet there it was, poised at the corner of the wooden frame, waiting for some fly to stray into its web.

As Jeannie rocked a swaddled baby, she wondered if—in the supposedly sterile atmosphere of the Hanover nursery—any prey would appear. Turning her eyes from the web, Jeannie examined the bundle in her arms. Nearly six weeks old and still under five pounds in weight. The little girl had a head like a fuzzy peach. Jeannie had fed her from a bottle with a special small-sized nipple. Though the baby was almost asleep, one tiny hand was curled around Jeannie's index finger.

As Jeannie hummed softly, words to describe the child shifted about inside her head. She arranged and re-arranged them in patterns. By lunchtime, she would be able to take a pen and put them on paper.

Because of Martin Storey, Jeannie had left Pediatrics to spend her Christmas vacation working in the nursery. With the gradual, gratifying disappearance of polio patients, her uncle had focused his attention on the medical problems of premature babies.

Martin and other doctors were working on a theory that it was bad for preemies to spend so much time by themselves in the incubators and bassinets of the nursery.

So, once again, Jeannie was a special case. Martin Storey's niece, allowed to provide extra hands for cuddling.

The yellow apron she had worn for the last two and a half years had faded to a warm cream color. Now it lay folded on the shelf of her closet, because in the nursery Jeannie wore sterile green operating-room garb and a gauze mask.

Here, her patients did not finger-paint or do jigsaw puzzles. They seldom cried. Preemies tended to be sleepy, she discovered. Part of her work was to stimulate them, encourage them to stay awake and respond to people.

Although much of her time was taken up with diapering, holding, feeding, she was learning. In the pediatric ward, she had begun to feel more like an occupational therapist than like a would-be doctor.

This was important to her. Each day when she came, she picked up some new technique or scrap of medical information. After a year of serious doubts, she had a new surge of interest in medicine. She needed that, too. The fall of her junior year had been a period of self-examination and doubts. In the nursery, she was finding more excitement than she had known in months.

The nursery staff was happy to have an extra pair of hands. Jeannie, at almost seventeen, didn't look like a child any more. No one treated her as Cabot once had. The nurses were demanding, but had faith that Jeannie would follow their instructions and care for the infants competently.

Still, they liked to tease her. They joked that Jeannie fed others yet forgot to feed herself. She was on the way to a belated lunch when her eye caught sight of something pinned to the outer set of nursery doors. It was a piece of white paper. Instead of being handwritten, the message had been typed on a machine with inky keys.

why me, why me, i have asked so many times over the last years, with never any words to answer. tested young, but have i met the test, have i answered that incomprehensible challenge? i am wondering, always wondering, when i see her and them, those who can walk free of this place, free of pain, who move with the rare unconscious grace of young giraffes, unknowing, uncaring, mute.

YETI

Jeannie was stunned. She wasn't sure what Kit was doing at Hanover or how he had known she was working in the nursery. Then it came to her. Kit must be having the long-awaited surgery on his left leg. And he knew where she was the same way he always did—through Martin Storey.

She had hardly seen or thought about Kit since the Winter Ball a year ago. When they passed in the halls, they tried not to look at each other. Kit no longer took pictures for the *Banner*. Messages from Yeti had ceased to appear.

Seeing a new message on the nursery door brought back Jeannie's old feelings of guilt about Kit, but at the same time it made her angry. She recognized now that Kit deliberately played on her sympathies. Though she was aware of this, she knew she was going to skip lunch and go find him.

In a way she couldn't define, she felt, as she had many times before, that she owed him this. He had reached out to her with his words. If she did not respond, she would show herself to be a cold, heartless person.

As she walked down the surgical corridor toward the room listed under his name, she had no notion what she was going to say. She paused outside the half-opened door. Then she knocked.

"Come in," a familiar voice called. It had a brisk yet not unfriendly tone.

When Jeannie stepped inside, she saw he had been waiting for her. Wearing his old plaid bathrobe, he was seated in a high-backed chair facing the door. On the lowered tray table was his typewriter and a stack of paper. He looked ready to spring at her. She was the unsuspecting fly in this hospital, the fly who was walking into a sticky trap.

Seeing her, Kit pushed the table aside and stood up. Jeannie looked around the room. He was in a double, but the other half was unoccupied. His bed was by the window. Rain slashed against it as she walked forward to shake his outstretched hand. Although he looked genuinely pleased to see her, she couldn't shake off the image of the web.

"*Silken yet strong,*" whispered the words inside her head. "*Iridescent cords web hands . . . in a white-mirrored maze . . .*"

"It's good to see you," Kit said in a voice that scattered the words in all directions.

"Hello, Kit," she answered. When she looked at him, she realized that he was several inches taller than she was now. His face had changed, too, had become more angular. "How are you?"

"How am I? Feeling like Pinocchio waiting for Gepetto to carve a new leg to replace the one that broke when I tumbled off a shelf."

Jeannie laughed. "You must have worked a long time on that one!"

"Not too long," he admitted. "So how are you?"

Standing on one foot, Jeannie took a moment to search for an appropriate answer. "Well . . . I feel nervous—like

Snow White in her glass coffin wondering . . . wondering if anyone is ever going to come and wake me up."

Kit chuckled appreciatively. "Not bad. A little trite, maybe."

Looking down, Jeannie noticed the bedroom slippers on his feet. "They haven't operated yet?"

"No, tomorrow morning early. I get to be Sunrise Classroom for the interns and residents. There aren't too many old polios around, so I get to be the big show of the week."

"Are you scared?"

Kit didn't answer the question. Instead, he pointed at her outfit, with the mask hanging loosely down the front. "By the look of you, Dr. West, you have completed your surgical training. Will I see you bending over me tomorrow morning when I'm waiting for them to put me to sleep?"

Jeannie looked down at her unflattering attire. "Nope. Sorry. I only do brain surgery. And, well, you do know— I'm wearing the operating greenies for the babies."

After a long pause, Kit asked a question. "How's Mike?"

"Mike who?" she asked, deliberately provoking him. This was the waiting web she had sensed. It wasn't so bad. She would be able to extricate herself.

"Mike O'Connor. Don't play games with me, you wonk. We know each other too well for that."

"Do we?" Jeannie asked.

Kit held up one hand. "Let's start this conversation over," he suggested, spreading a veneer of pleasantness over his irritation. "How is Michael O'Connor?"

"All right. Editing the *Banner*—but you know that. Look, Kit, Mike and I haven't gone out since last spring. He takes out Lisabeth now. And it's okay—we're all friends." She was offering him some information about the last year of her life, but she was holding back, too.

"Anyone new?"

"No. I've been working hard this year—being a grind, I guess. Spending a lot of time by myself. Maybe too much. Maybe it makes me boring."

Kit took what she said without displaying much emotion, yet Jeannie could see he was interested to hear she was spending time alone, that she had no new person in her life. There had never been anything romantic between Kit and herself. She doubted that there ever would be.

He still had too much fierceness about him, too much anger. She did not think she wanted to put up with that again. Talking with him was all right, though, even enjoyable.

"You climbing?" she asked, aware that she did not care about his answer but that he would want her to inquire.

"Some," he said, bending over to take hold of a cane. "Dmitri and I—with a few other guys—have formed a climbing club." Here Kit paused to laugh. "It's the Climbing and Charlie Parker Club. But we call ourselves the Birdmen."

Jeannie smiled without knowing why. "Who's Charlie Parker?"

Kit pounded the tip of the cane against the floor. "Who's Charlie Parker, she asks. Only the world's greatest jazz sax. Well, how would you know? Anyway, it's been good—rocks and jazz, interesting and a lot better than the sock-hop wonkiness which affects everyone at Jackson."

The note of superiority in Kit's voice bothered Jeannie, but she had to agree. She was jealous that he was finding something distinctive in a school that offered her less and less.

"After the surgery," he continued, caught up in his

enthusiasm, "there will be more therapy. Back to the old marbles. But then, if I'm lucky, maybe I'll have enough strength in my leg to do some real climbing. I'm hoping."

Jeannie liked the way Kit sounded. Instead of the crazed obsession about Yosemite and Half Dome, he was speaking sensibly. She was, at that moment, sorry they hadn't stayed friends after last year's Winter Ball.

"Mmm . . . Kit?" she said, hating herself for her tentative tone. She had worked hard to get rid of that persistent lack of confidence. Trying to make her voice stronger, she continued. "Do you have to stay here? In the room?"

He examined her suspiciously. "No. The lab work's already finished. As long as I don't roller-skate in the rain, I guess I'm free."

"Well . . . I thought maybe you'd have a milk shake with me down in the cafeteria."

Kit didn't answer immediately. He seemed to enjoy watching her squirm at his hesitation.

When they had bought their milk shakes, Jeannie picked up the tray. Kit, using his cane for balance, followed as she made her way toward a window table.

Before they reached it, an unmistakable voice accosted them from behind. Strident, with a slight German accent. Sylvia Goldberger. "Jeanne-Marie and Christopher," she said, "how nice to know that two young people can enjoy a soda together even in the inhospitable environment of a hospital."

After sipping some milk shake from the top of an overflowing cup, Jeannie turned to greet the therapist. There was more gray showing in her hair, but she was, as always, wearing a bright dress under her drooping lab coat. Jeannie and Kit both towered over her now.

"Have you seen Mrs. Cabot?" Dr. Goldberger asked.

"That would be, I think, a very considerate thing to do while you are both here together."

Kit didn't look unhappy to see Dr. Goldberger, yet the idea of visiting Old-Death-and-Dying obviously held no great charm for him. "If I went to Pediatrics," he said, "I'd be going to see Alonzo."

When no one made any comment, Kit kept talking. "Alonzo means a lot to me. When I was here, he did things for me, talked about baseball, kept me company . . ."

Jeannie sent a pleading look in Dr. Goldberger's direction. Then the doctor put a hand on Kit's shoulder. "Alonzo is dead," she said gently. "A heart attack. Maybe six months ago. Jeanne-Marie and I—we knew this already. I am sorry, Christopher."

Kit looked desolate, and then furious. The conversation with Dr. Goldberger was over. Jeannie said the goodbyes. She found them a table and insisted that they sit, but she had no idea how to help.

"Why," Kit moaned, hitting the table with his fist, "didn't I go back more? See him more? I don't think I ever really thanked him for all the things he did for me."

"I wrote a poem about him once," she said quietly. That was all she had to offer. "A poem about Alonzo and you—about friendship."

Kit looked up fiercely. "Since when do you write poetry?"

"Since last year."

Alonzo was forgotten as Kit stared at her from across the table. "I always knew you were a poet. When can I see something? This week—after my surgery—I'll be flat on my back and have plenty of time to read."

Jeannie drew back. She was not writing for anyone but herself. Impulse had made her speak up. She had never meant to mention her poems.

"Come on, Jeannie. Promise me you'll show me—especially the one about Alonzo. Promise."

Hesitant, Jeannie stalled for time. "Well . . ."

"Promise me, please. I won't make comments. I'd just like to look at it. Listen, Alonzo was . . . he meant something and—come on, you see what *I* write."

Frowning, she licked the tip of her straw. Kit had never referred to the Yeti messages before.

"All right," she agreed. "Yes. Or maybe. Oh, Kit, I really don't know."

"Jeannie?"

"What?"

"Alonzo was . . ." A strange hoarse sound escaped from the back of Kit's throat. Jeannie looked up.

He was crying. "It was Alonzo who taped up the Yeti messages for me when I was here. That's how they went up so mysteriously. No one saw him. He was an orderly—an invisible person. I saw him then, but I forgot. Forgot and didn't come back."

"Oh, Kit," Jeannie said helplessly. "Oh, Kit." As she was reaching out, as she was clumsily overturning her milk shake, she suspected—even if it took time—that she would show him her poetry.

12

$\mathcal{O}$N THE following day, Jeannie left the nursery promptly at noon. Then she headed straight up to Kit's room. From the hallway she could see that his blinds were drawn and that the room was dark. As she had done before, she hesitated in the doorway and knocked.

"Enter," a woman's voice called out.

Jeannie went in. Kit was flat on his back, looking like the wooden puppet to which he had compared himself. He was breathing heavily, sleeping off the effects of general anesthesia. Seated in the chair next to the bed was a large-breasted woman wearing a navy-blue dress with a white collar. It was Kit's mother.

"I wanted to find out how Kit is doing," Jeannie said nervously.

As Mrs. Hayden examined her, Jeannie wished she had thought to remove the greenies. She would have looked more presentable in her own clothes. Kit's mother was entirely presentable-looking. In fact, she looked almost as if she felt underdressed because she had forgotten a veiled hat and white kid gloves.

"Are you an employee?" Kit's mother asked. The woman's voice had a cultured Eastern sort of cadence.

"No, I'm Jeannie West. I go to school with Kit. At Jackson. I'm just a volunteer here."

"Speak up," the woman urged firmly. " 'Wake Duncan

with thy knocking, would you could.' That is to say—Kit is out cold. We could tap dance on the end of the bed without being in danger of awakening him."

Jeannie looked over at Kit. A foot guard attached to the end of his bed had a white blanket draped over it, keeping his leg from having to bear the weight of the covers. "When will they know?" she asked, raising her voice, "if the operation has been a success?"

"When do they ever know anything? How did I get caught in the middle of this? Eleanor's so normal. Doing so well at U.C.L.A. Let me tell you, having a child with a chronic disability is—oh, but you're just a child. Forgive me. I forget myself."

As Jeannie stood licking her lips, she was aware of a sick-sweet smell in the room. Wondering about it, she also wondered how it would be to have this person for a mother. Mrs. Hayden made Jeannie feel like Alice being lectured by the Red Queen. The next thing she knew, she would be urged to do six impossible things before breakfast every morning.

"Do you have any notion of what it is like," the woman went on, choosing to forget Jeannie's age again, "to live with the continual pressure of—"

Her sentence was never finished because a voice from the doorway interrupted it. "Tish, don't get worked up, please. Let's stay calm. Chin up. Be prepared."

Jeannie turned halfway around. The man behind her, compact and slender, with a small, clipped moustache, was Kit's father. "How do you do," she said, beginning all over again. "I'm Jeannie West. A friend of Kit's."

"Pleased to know you, my dear. Are you a Girl Scout?"

"No," she answered, thinking that there was something peculiar about the question and about Kit's parents. Mr. Hayden's look seemed to imply that she had something wrong with her if she wasn't a Scout.

"Well, my son is not a Scout, either. Although, naturally, by now he would have probably been an Eagle."

Kit's mother rose to her feet. "Fritz, shall we go out for a while? Perhaps the grill down the street. And perhaps this young woman will volunteer to sit with Kit while we step out."

"Of course. You go on, and I'll stay here." It didn't occur to Jeannie to tell them that she was expected back in the nursery by one.

As the Haydens were leaving, Jeannie walked toward the door with them. It was then she realized that the sick-sweet smell wasn't clinging to Kit but to his mother. While she strained to identify it, Kit's father looked her over. "Rather an attractive filly, Tish," he commented, making Jeannie wonder if she should open her mouth and let him examine her teeth as if she were a horse being offered for sale. "Not Eleanor, of course, but—"

"Fritz," Mrs. Hayden snapped. "That is enough. And you, my dear," she continued, changing the tone in her voice, "we appreciate your kindness."

With those words they were gone, and Jeannie was left alone with Kit. As she turned back toward him, she knew what that smell was. Though her own parents didn't drink much, she was aware that Mrs. Hayden's breath exuded fumes from gin or vodka—one of those clear liquors people drank when they didn't want anyone to know they were drinking.

Jeannie was still mulling this over when Kit spoke. His voice was thick, and he did not attempt to open his eyes. "I am loyal, brave, reverent, clean, and kind, but I am not a Boy Scout. With my shrunken-up leg, I'd look lousy in their short pants."

"What are you talking about?"

"He works for them," Kit mumbled.

Jeannie was confused. "Who works for whom? Have you been listening all this time?"

"My dad—for the Scouts. Part of it, drifting," he told her, attempting to answer both questions at once.

"You never told me," she said. Then she remembered his leg. "Does it hurt?"

"Dull. But I'm still drunk as a skunk on morphine. Like Bird and the other jazzmen, I'm flying through clouds and near mountains . . . beautiful."

Jeannie didn't say anything. She leaned on the bedside table, putting her elbows near the typewriter. It had a piece of paper in it, but the paper was blank. She wished Kit would open his eyes.

A moment or two later, he did. His pupils were huge and had the unfocused look of a newborn. "Father said you are an attractive filly, Jeannie with the light-brown hair. And Father, when he isn't obsessed by scouting, has excellent taste."

She could feel herself flush in response to his words. "How come you never said anything like that when you weren't drunk on morphine?"

"Imhib . . . I mean, I'm imhib . . . inhibited, shy and anyway . . ."

"Because it's shallow," Jeannie suggested, remembering how Yeti's message had compared her to a sluggish, shallow creek. "Placing importance on looks is shallow, and you don't like to admit you do it, too."

She thought that Kit winked at her, yet it happened so quickly that she couldn't be sure. "Oh, yes, you have turned into a looker, Jeannie West," he said, using distinctly uncharacteristic language.

"Same old scarecrow," she protested mildly. "Anyway, you're sloshed."

Sighing, he closed his eyes. "No more scarecrow. Try a

109

mirror. It can tell you as well as I can," he murmured, dropping his voice. "And I'm not the one who's sloshed. Well, now that you've met them, do you like me better or worse?"

"Who?"

"Mother and Father. My beloved parents."

Jeannie chose not to answer the question. She expected that Kit might open his eyes and challenge her. Instead, he drifted off again into the stupor of the anesthesia. He was still sleeping at one-twenty when his parents returned.

As Jeannie pulled on a fresh set of greenies, she worried that Kit was, once again, going to complicate her life. But there was no time to brood. The nursery staff was frantic because they were about to lose Jon, a five-day-old preemie with a breathing problem. Hyaline membrane disease. Jon's parents stood helplessly at the glass window. A call had been put in for Martin Storey.

At the same time, someone had to prepare a dimpled three-month-old named Cindy for discharge. Having kept her weight above five pounds for three consecutive days, she could go home. Jeannie was sorry to see her going. Cindy had even begun to smile.

When Martin Storey hurried in to examine Jon, he was grim-faced. He listened to the infant's chest with his stethoscope, massaged the tiny body. Watching Martin, remembering Kit downstairs, she asked herself all over again why it was she believed she wanted to be a doctor. Children still died. They were still crippled by disease or marked by genetic deficiencies.

After the immediate crisis had subsided, and Jon was back in the incubator, she went to speak with her uncle. "Martin?"

"Yes, my pet?"

"Is Jon going to make it?"

Her uncle mopped his forehead with a clean diaper. "No. No—he's not. Not a thing that modern medicine has devised will keep that precious boy alive."

Then Martin fell silent, absorbed by his own thoughts. A moment later, his mood shifted. "Jeannie, my girl, I understand that Kit has come through with flying colors. Glick—the surgeon—says he believes the muscle transplant went well, that all is quite satisfactory."

Jeannie smiled. Good news was welcome. "Does that mean that he might really be well? Be fine, be able to climb again?"

"Oh, no—not you, too! I have to go back to work. To an office overflowing with runny noses waiting for a doctor's Kleenex. I don't have time for all this talk about climbing. Can't you find something useful to do?"

Stung by her uncle's tone of voice, Jeannie spent the afternoon doing all the worst tasks in the nursery. She didn't know whether Martin had been angry with her, with Kit, or with the irreversible fact that a five-day-old boy was about to die.

At three, when her workday was over, Jeannie changed into her own skirt and blouse. On impulse, she decided to check on Kit, hoping his parents would be gone, hoping he would be awake. She paused only momentarily to wonder why, if she didn't want him in her life, she kept going up to see him.

As she stepped out of the elevator on the fourth floor with this question unanswered, the first thing she heard was a voice, husky and loud. Kit's mother was in the hall by the nurses' station. On the floor at her feet was her pocketbook—its contents strewn on the linoleum.

"Stolen," Mrs. Hayden shouted, twisting from side to side so that her bosom heaved and the navy pleats in her dress swirled like an upside-down tornado. "Twenty dollars stolen while I was watching my son. My son who is a polio victim. I am being nibbled to death by rabbits. Always nibbled by rabbits. Twenty dollars stolen!"

Jeannie backed up against the wall, something she hadn't done at Hanover since she'd been a timid fourteen-year-old. As Mrs. Hayden shouted about rabbits and stolen money, Kit's father tugged at her elbow. "Time to go, Tish. Come on, stiff upper lip. Shoulders back. We must go now."

A young orderly bent down and stuffed Mrs. Hayden's belongings into her purse. When Mr. Hayden took hold of the purse and guided his wife into the elevator, Jeannie pressed herself firmly against the stippled plaster. She was afraid that if she were discovered, she'd be accused of stealing the twenty dollars.

After what she had witnessed, she no longer wanted to see Kit. For a long time, she stood in the hall debating with herself. Then, at last, she headed on toward his room.

Pausing outside, she knocked. "Kit?"

He didn't answer. She knocked and called again. There was still no response. Deciding not to wait for one, she tiptoed in. Kit was, as he had been before, on his back, lying stiffly with his eyes closed.

Jeannie walked to the side of the bed. Kit didn't move. He was quiet. Too quiet. He was, she realized, desperately embarrassed by the scene his mother had just caused. Unwilling to admit he was awake, he was probably wishing he could make her disappear like an inconvenient rabbit.

She would have liked to say something reassuring. But remembering Anna Dorado's ability to keep quiet if there was nothing to be said, she held her tongue. Kit was suffering enough. No words of hers could comfort him. She understood some of his anger better than she had before, yet she was never going to discuss his mother unless he brought up the subject first.

She was turning to walk from the room when she noticed that the piece of paper in the typewriter was no longer blank.

> *consumed i am with ugly green envy as i see her easy grace and know she has an easy, loving family. then i feel pain not of the body but the inner pain of longing, the pain of wanting to be near something so lovely, unfragile and whole, hoping that nearness might make me less unlovely, less fragile, more whole. when i cry out, does she hear?*
>
> *YETI*

Brushing one hand across her eyes, Jeannie glanced at Kit. He was beginning to shake uncontrollably. Jeannie wasn't sure if he was crying, cold, or suffering aftereffects from anesthesia.

If Kit had been small, she would have scooped him up in her arms and rocked him like one of the newborns. But he wasn't and she couldn't. Settling for the only reasonable thing she could do, she took an extra blanket from the shelf of his closet and covered him lightly. She was about to go look for a nurse when something else occurred to her.

Bending over Kit's typewriter, she typed one word. *Yes.* Then, without glancing back, she left.

13

Because it was Christmas Eve, Jeannie dressed in red —her favorite kilt with a new cherry-colored sweater and a string of pearls. She wanted to look nice. Although she was not scheduled to work, she was going to Hanover to bring a present to Kit.

Though they had seen one another a few times since the surgery on his leg, it was always with his mother hovering nearby. Whatever problems Mrs. Hayden had with alcohol, she appeared to be fiercely devoted to Kit and to his welfare.

Today Jeannie would not be seeing her or Kit's father, because they were down in Carmel visiting relatives. Jeannie was glad that she and Kit were finally going to have a chance to talk without a chaperone.

When Jeannie reached his room, however, no one was there. Nor had he left any message for her on the bed or in the typewriter. As she was standing there wondering what to do, a pony-tailed nurse looked in from the hall.

"If you are Jean, Kit said you'd find him up in Pediatrics. He said you know your way."

Puzzled, Jeannie left Kit's present next to the typewriter and went down to the ward. As she came through the doorway, the first thing she noticed was Santa Claus. He was sitting in a wheelchair. Slung over the back of the chair was a huge sack; and he was rolling from bed to bed dispensing gifts along with ho-ho-hos. Her uncle usually dressed in that costume, but the man in the wheelchair was not Martin Storey. *He* wouldn't have been traveling about the ward by wheelchair. A string of silk scarves confirmed that she was watching Santa Kit, cruising in his stainless-steel sleigh.

Leaning against the doorway, she noticed that he gave time to everyone, even the children still trapped in iron lungs. She never ceased to be amazed that Kit, who could be so angry and impatient, had developed such patience with the children.

Jeannie shifted her attention to them. In only a few weeks away from the ward, she had forgotten how desperate, how ill many of the children were. The bandages, the IVs, the dark circles under young eyes. Yet she was hearing sounds of excitement and laughter. Santa was obviously good medicine for sick children.

As she stood there, Cabot marched up. "So where have you been?" she asked in her usual manner.

Jeannie smiled. She was used to Cabot. "In the nursery. Well . . . you know that. I saw you last week trying to help with Jon."

"That's not what I mean. It wouldn't hurt, you know, to stop here sometimes and see old friends. They miss you."

"You're right. Well . . . Jon died. We've been busy and—"

"It's action I'm looking for. Not excuses."

Jeannie frowned. She had not come to Hanover on Christmas Eve to be bullied by Cabot. She had come to see Kit. But he was caught up in the festivities in Pediatrics, and she was left with Old-Death-and-Dying. Just as she was about to say something rude to the gray-haired nurse, Kit came spinning over to where they were.

"Merry Christmas, Merry Christmas!" he cried, imitating a deep-voiced, big-bellied man.

"Hi," Jeannie said.

"And have you been a good girl this year?"

Jeannie's irritation with Cabot plus the sense that Kit was deliberately avoiding time alone with her oozed out in her tone of voice. "If I sit in your lap and tell you I'm a good girl, do I get a candy cane?"

"You look like a candy cane," he said, bringing back memories of another day when he had seen her in that skirt and called her a peppermint.

"Well, you look like an overripe tomato that should be tossed in the spaghetti sauce. How come *you're* Santa Claus?"

"Your uncle Martin," Kit whispered with a mock air of resignation. "Who else?" Then he leaned closer to her. "Listen, this Santa routine is wearing a little thin, and I need some help. I promised the kids entertainment—a ballerina."

"You're not serious? Yes, you are. Well, forget it, because I'm no ballerina any more. You know that."

"What about the dance club at school?"

"Modern dance. And a club. That's different."

"Not to me," Kit insisted, "since I don't dance at all. Now, Mrs. Cabot—the music, please!"

Before Jeannie could stop her, Cabot put a scratchy recording of Tchaikovsky's *Nutcracker Suite* on the ward phonograph, and Kit was reintroducing her to the children.

"Jeannie—the peppermint lady—is here, girls and boys. We have a dancing candy cane to dance with you. And here we go!"

She would have argued with Kit, but she was not willing to make a scene in front of the children. Reluctantly, she pulled off her loafers and knee socks.

At first she was awkward, acutely conscious of her height and of their assortment of physical disabilities.

Gradually, she relaxed. Soon she ceased to be angry with Kit, forgot to be self-conscious. Then she was spinning and spinning as part of a ring of dancing children.

Moving lightly, she waltzed to the music. She lifted a few of the smaller patients and swung them through the air in time to the dreamy music. Her feet danced, her body moved until she was conscious of nothing except the sound of the music and the faces of the children.

The ambulatory ones danced with her as she twirled from place to place. For the ones who could not get up from their beds, she offered fleeting handshakes and butterfly kisses. Cabot had vanished. Kit was nowhere to be seen. Never, even when she was twelve or thirteen and dancing with the Pacific Ballet, had she felt so free as she danced. It was a feeling she wanted to cling to, something she did not want to lose. Surrounded by bright eyes and rows of tiny white milk teeth, she was flying.

After a while, a tinge of sadness seeped into her consciousness. The minor key of the music reminded her that many of these children would never get well, that others would never be whole again. Then she shook off those thoughts. Again she felt wonderful. For the moment, Kit had worked magic.

Suddenly, though, the record was over. Jeannie stopped.

"I'm going to flip it to the second side," Cabot announced.

Jeannie shook her head. She was out of breath. She knew she couldn't recapture her excitement or summon the energy for another side of the *Nutcracker*.

"Sorry, really sorry," she said, panting.

The children pulled at her and pleaded, but she shook her head. "Ask Santa Claus for more tricks."

Kit wheeled up close behind her. "Welcome back," he said heartily.

"From where?"

"From whatever galaxy you were spinning through. You looked like a brilliant red meteor."

Still breathless, she turned and began to laugh. "And you look like—oh, forget it. I'm not up to that now."

Though she was laughing, she was embarrassed, shy. She had never admitted to Kit how much dancing meant to her. Maybe she hadn't admitted it to herself. But he had just seen it, and his face—even under the false beard —told her he would not forget. She felt as if she were standing before him wearing only her string of pearls.

"Jeannie, come back! Listen—I've arranged for a surprise. Come back to earth and listen to me."

"What kind of surprise?"

"We can go out to lunch. To the grill down the block. As long as I go in my chair. No weight on my foot until next week. But we have a pass. It's legal."

Jeannie liked the idea, yet she was self-conscious, slow to respond. After all, Kit had just seen her dancing wildly through the ward.

"And I've invited Cabot to come along."

"Cabot!" Jeannie started to giggle nervously.

"Listen, it's Christmas Eve, and she doesn't have anyone. Look, after the way I forgot about Alonzo, I figured —well, anyway, I asked her. You don't mind, do you?"

Of course, she didn't mind. If Cabot was there to chaperone them, Jeannie would not have to figure out why she was suddenly warm and nervous at the idea of being alone with him.

While Kit was changing from the Santa Claus suit, Jeannie went to the rest room to wash her perspiring face. Instead of attempting to deal with her own mixed-up emotions, she tried to observe herself objectively in the mirror. She saw flushed cheeks, which might have been the result of half an hour of frenzied dancing.

Or of her new shyness with Kit. But, in any case, the girl facing her looked all right.

That girl, the light-haired boy, and the formidable nurse made something of a stir as they came into the Shamrock Grill. Its ceiling and walls were hung with garlands of fir tied with red ribbons. A fire was in the fireplace, and the luncheon special was turkey with cranberry sauce. Once they were seated at a table, it was hard to realize that, outside, the air was still California mild instead of cold and snowy.

All three ordered the special, but after that they sat in embarrassed silence. For a while, as Cabot sipped the bourbon she'd ordered, they tried to talk about the Christmas party in the ward.

Then, instead of getting better, things got worse. Kit asked Jeannie a question about her poetry. As she sent a cold look in his direction, icy words skated inside her head, trying to express how alarming it was to hear him tell someone like Cabot that she wrote poems.

Cabot, however, didn't show any interest in whether Jeannie did or did not write. By the time the meals were placed in front of them, she had taken charge of the conversation. She told them all about her late husband and about a six-year-old child she had lost to diphtheria. Tears welled up in Jeannie's eyes. All of a sudden, she understood that Cabot saw her own son again every time she stood beside the bed of someone else's dying child.

After a while, Jeannie glanced over at Kit. Instead of sharing her feelings of sympathy for Cabot, he was scowling. His eyes watched disapprovingly as she began a second glass of bourbon. Cabot, oblivious to his disapproval, told further anecdotes about her husband and son, but Kit did not seem to hear her.

Suddenly he pulled out the money his mother had

given him to pay for lunch. With impatience, he urged them to finish. "I'm tired," he insisted. "I want to get back to bed."

The rest of the meal was short and silent. Soon they were heading for the door. It was then that Jeannie noticed for the first time how people turned their eyes so they wouldn't have to look at Kit in the wheelchair.

Only one man gazed directly down on him. "What's the matter, sonny?" he asked in a well-meaning way. "Break your leg?"

"No," Kit answered glumly. "I had polio."

"I thought no one got that any more," the man said, stricken.

"They don't," Kit told him.

With that exchange fresh in her head, Jeannie followed Kit and Cabot silently back to the hospital. Cabot said her thank yous and goodbyes in the elevator. As soon as she had stepped out, Kit spoke. "I hate to see people drinking."

Jeannie wanted to protest that Cabot had not been drunk, only relaxed by the alcohol. She wanted to tell him that she knew now that Cabot was human, even likable in ways; yet she was not strong enough to stand up to Kit's rage over the subject of drinking. His reaction, though, gave her some idea of how terrible it must be to have a parent who might stage an irrational scene at any time.

Jeannie was beginning to wish she was back home by herself when Kit caught sight of her present. "What's that?" he asked as he wheeled into his room.

"A surprise," she said. "From me."

"Can I open it now? Is that all right? Or must I wait?"

"Open it," Jeannie told him, happy to see that his mood had changed.

Hopping on one foot, Kit moved from the wheelchair to the bed. Then he tore into the neat, holly-patterned paper with which Jeannie had wrapped the present. Inside, he found a notebook bound in green leather.

Without cracking it open, he turned the book in his hands, fingering the smooth binding. "Is this really for me?" he asked in an unfamiliar boyish manner.

Jeannie nodded. Even without an explanation, he appeared to know why she had selected this notebook for him. Yet, when he opened it, he seemed surprised to find the pages blank. He riffled through the whole book as if he were searching for something. Finally he looked up. "It's empty."

"Of course."

"Why is it empty?"

"So you can fill it," she said, "with your messages—with whatever you have to say. Keep a journal of your work instead of only messages that get lost."

Kit sighed. "Look, when I saw this, I thought you were keeping your promise to me, going to show me some of your poems."

Jeannie wanted to leave, but she didn't. At the mention of her poetry, she threw her hands in the air. "Oh, Kit, Kit, I never made such a promise. Well, maybe I did, but if I did I didn't mean it. My poems are private. I told you that—told you they were personal."

Suddenly she did not have any self-restraint left. "You don't listen to me. When we talked about Alonzo, you pushed me into saying I'd show you my stuff. Today you pushed me into dancing when I didn't want—"

"—and you loved it."

"That's beside the point. You push me. You're always pushing me. This doesn't work. We seem to bring out the worst in each other!"

"That's not true," he said. "And you know it."

She knew it, yet she felt confused. She was, once again, as warm and nervous as she'd been before lunch.

"Why is it?" she asked. "Why can't we just—just . . . be civilized? Why can't we just *talk?*"

Kit stared at her until she began to squirm. "Because we can't."

The tension in the room made her feel like a cattail about to snap in a furious wind. "But why not? What's going on?"

He tossed the notebook into her hands. "If you can't figure it out for yourself, Jeannie West, I'm sure as hell not going to tell you!"

14

$\mathscr{J}$EANNIE refused to look up and admit she had caught sight of Kit. Propped up on a pair of crutches, he was peering through the nursery window, watching her. Ever since Christmas Eve, she had avoided him. She was not willing to keep working at a friendship that was breaking apart for reasons he seemed to understand and she did not.

Continuing to ignore him, she concentrated her attention on a newborn named Andrew—a blue baby who had undergone heart surgery to keep him alive. As Jeannie helped a nurse change the dressing, she could see that the child still had a slight bluish tinge to his face. He was going to have a long scar across his chest. She wondered if Andrew, like Kit, would grow up angry at being different.

No matter how hard she tried, Jeannie wasn't able to put Kit out of her mind. He was like a kaleidoscope. She never knew from one turn to another whether the patterns she saw would be bright and beautiful or dark and muddied.

As Jeannie thought about Kit, he kept staring at her through the viewing window. He stood there so long that the nurses started to notice him.

Finally, one of them scooped up Andrew. "Get out of here," the woman said teasingly. "It's your lunchtime. And I think that big boy out there needs you more 'n this little one here."

A knowing wave of laughter rippled through the nursery, and Kit's company suddenly seemed to be a lesser threat than staying to be quizzed about who he was.

When she came through the double doors to meet him, she was ill at ease, irritable. "What do you want?" she asked.

"I have a Christmas present for you," he said. "It's late, but I haven't seen you. Where have you been?"

She frowned. "Here. At home. If you wanted to reach me, you know how. You could have come sooner. You could have called."

"Hey—whoa. You're like a pickle left too long in a vat of salt."

"And you," she replied without hesitation, "are like a persimmon that looks good but has the same sour taste every time. And—don't worry about a present. Whatever it is, I don't think I want it."

"Mercy, Jeannie. Show some mercy for me." Kit leaned forward on his crutches. He slumped his head. "Listen, you're right. I'm sorry I was hard on Cabot, hard on you. Look—can't we start over?"

Despite herself, she laughed. "We are always starting over. Haven't you noticed?"

Kit laughed, too. "I've noticed. But we are friends again, aren't we? Come to P.T. with me—come see Syl Goldberger, and after I'm through, I'll tell you all about your present."

When Kit was as gentle with her as he was with the young children, she found him irresistible. Even though she was going to miss lunch, she agreed to come watch his physical therapy.

Sylvia Goldberger seemed pleased yet not particularly surprised to see her. As always at Hanover, Jeannie had the impression that everyone knew everything. She wasn't going to miss lunch, either. Dr. Goldberger had a sandwich and two apples on her desk. "Help yourself, Jeanne-Marie," she said. "We shall share our midday meal as Christopher struggles."

And struggle he did. Jeannie had never watched Kit working in P.T. before. If Dr. Goldberger once had to spur him harder by demanding that he "work harder, dammit," that was no longer necessary. With little assistance from her, he proceeded to put his crutches aside and warm up on the mats with a series of stretching exercises. Because his left leg was in a cast, he was trying to be careful with it. Yet, whenever he pulled it too hard or moved it too quickly, he winced with pain.

If Kit's therapy in this room had ever consisted, as he used to proclaim, mostly of picking up marbles with his toes, it did not any more. Now he worked with weights and levers, exerting himself with frightening intensity. As Jeannie took bites from a tuna-fish sandwich, she realized he was concentrating so hard he had forgotten she was there. Sweat poured off his face, trickling through his hair, making it even curlier than usual.

As soon as he was finished with the weights, he moved to the rings and parallel bars. Occasionally, he grunted and asked the therapist, whom he now called Syl, a question about balance or technique; yet for the most part he was absorbed, shut off, struggling to make himself strong.

Jeannie looked at his left leg. She could tell that, underneath its cast, it was still abnormally thin. As Kit worked to build it up, he was as lost in his world as she had been while dancing to the *Nutcracker*. This boy she was watching was not doing mindless exercises in a hospital gym. He was climbing step by step up the face of Half Dome. And he didn't care if she knew it.

Near the end of the session, as Kit swung on the parallel bars, his hand—wet with sweat—slipped. He lost his balance. His left ankle bent sideways. Only a quick swipe of his hand kept him from falling onto the mat.

Dr. Goldberger did not react to the slip but continued to peel an apple with the small knife she had produced from the pocket of her lab coat. Jeannie resisted an impulse to rush forward and assure Kit that it was all right. As far as he was concerned, it was *not* all right.

"Dammit," he cried out to no one in particular. He renewed his work on the bars with great vigor. "I'm so damn sick and tired of hurting, of being lame!" Then he let out a loud scream.

His concentration was gone. He seemed to have no energy left. He yelled again, making the whole room echo with his sense of frustration and failure.

"Christopher, in one way or another, we are all handicapped," Dr. Goldberger said. "Now, you would perhaps like to have a slice of apple?"

Fiercely, he glared at her. "No, what I would perhaps like," he replied, imitating her softly accented voice, "is a new leg."

"I am sorry," she answered. "New legs are only distributed on Walpurgis Night by demons who take your soul in exchange."

Kit's face brightened. "Not bad," he said, looking over at Jeannie. "With a little practice, Dr. Syl could be as good as you. Maybe she's a secret poet, too."

"Cut it out," Jeannie warned.

"Stop being so sensitive," Kit snapped back.

Sylvia Goldberger shook her head at both of them. Although her eyes reflected amusement, her voice kept its usual firm, cool tone. "Children, children. 'Every limit is a beginning as well as an ending.' Christopher, I dismiss you today with that quotation. It is from the works of a great writer, an Englishwoman named George Eliot. Instead of wishing for new legs, remember that. And treat Jeanne-Marie with respect. She seems to me to be a young woman worth pursuing."

Jeannie flushed. She never thought of herself as being pursued by Kit or, for that matter, worth pursuing.

"Of course," Dr. Goldberger continued as she walked the two of them toward the door, "I should be over-whelmed to feel that a young man with Christopher's qualities would be interested in me."

Then they were in the corridor alone. Jeannie was writhing with embarrassment and suspected Kit felt the same as he hobbled along on his crutches. Keeping her own steps short, she walked at his side, looking down at the trail of blue footprints on the floor.

She was shaken up by the idea that Kit might be inter-ested in her. She and Kit had been squabbling for so long that it had never before occurred to her that he liked her as a girl friend. They had talked. He had tried to influ-ence her, to impress her with his writing, encourage her to write, but that was all.

She was, at that moment, unable to speak. Then Kit's elbow poked her, and she jumped as if she had been burned by the tip of a glowing cigarette. If he was think-ing about her, he did not say so. She was aware of the faint locker-room aroma clinging to him as a result of his workout. Nothing he could do at this moment would surprise her—even if he let out another horrible yell. She felt his tension. The rubber tips of his crutches squealed against the linoleum.

Her hands were sticky. Glancing over at Kit, she thought she wanted to reach out and punch him. But she also wanted to throw her arms around him. She swal-lowed hard. Her thoughts were crazy, out of control.

She did not know how to deal with the prickling sensa-tion in her fingers and toes. Being around Mike O'Connor had never made her feel so strange. Without knowing why, she was afraid.

When she reached to press the elevator button, Kit finally spoke. He sounded hoarse, breathless. "I have tickets for the ballet—the *Nutcracker*—and I'd like you to go with me, if you want."

Before Jeannie found her voice, the elevator door opened, and the two of them walked in. The doors closed behind them, but neither one moved to push the button. They just stood there. When Jeannie raised her head, she found that Kit was staring at her.

"Jeannie." His voice was almost inaudible.

"What?" she asked, still afraid.

Kit was standing close to her. His eyes were asking silent questions. She was confused, not sure what the answers were.

"Jeannie," he repeated.

"Mmm?" she answered, aware that the elevator was moving, though neither of them had pushed a button.

It was then that she closed her eyes. As she did, she felt his lips touch hers. A soft touch with the flavor of salt. Kit only pulled away when the elevator doors parted. Jeannie could hear someone else enter. She opened her eyes, but she looked at Kit instead of toward the new passenger. She wondered if the two of them were going to stay in the elevator for the rest of the day, riding up and down, staring into each other's eyes.

"Jeannie," he said again, examining her face and also ignoring the elevator's third passenger.

"Yes?"

"Do you mind that I'm crippled?"

Several other people boarded, an audience for the small drama Kit and Jeannie were acting out in one corner of the moving elevator.

"We're all handicapped," she answered, quoting Dr. Goldberger.

Kit nodded. He moved closer to her again. Expectantly, she licked her lips, thinking how it was going to feel when he kissed her again, wondering if she dared put her arms around him.

" 'Every limit is a beginning,' " he said, quoting the therapist quoting George Eliot. "And we are, Jeannie, at a beginning. And—I'm scared."

With the fingertips of her left hand she brushed his cheek. "Me, too," she admitted. "But, about the ballet, if you mean it, if you want me to—I'd love to go with you. I—"

Her rush of speech was silenced as he leaned forward again. When the other passengers applauded both their words and the kiss that followed, they hardly noticed.

15

JEANNIE was excited about going to the ballet with Kit. It would have seemed more like a date if they were seeing the *Nutcracker* at night, but Mrs. Hayden had selected the tickets. She had chosen a matinee so that Kit and Jeannie could come back and have tea with her after the performance.

"Tea!" Jill exclaimed, as she helped zip her sister into a brown-and-white tweed dress. "How ritzy."

Jeannie slipped into her high-heeled pumps. "Well, the Haydens are from back East somewhere, and that's how they do things."

Jill, who was thirteen and only a year from entering high school, walked around examining Jeannie with a critical eye. "You look okay—but kind of mousy. Why didn't you wear the turquoise with the velvet?"

As Jeannie brushed her hair onto her shoulders, she was only half listening. She liked the warm tones of brown. Today Kit wouldn't tell her she looked like a piece of candy. A brown dress, she thought, was suitable for a poet. In its pocket, folded into little triangles, was one of her poems—a poem about dancing. She was going to give it to Kit.

Ever since they had kissed in the hospital elevator, all she wanted to do was be with him. Yet, no matter how she arranged her schedule, there never seemed to be enough time.

Now that Kit was out of the hospital, Jeannie hoped to change all that. Starting immediately. Kit had a walking cast and was, for the first time, able to get along without a crutch or a cane. He could drive, too. He was borrowing his family's car to take them to the Opera House. Learning that he drove—that he had been driving for a year—was only one of many new things she was discovering about him.

All the way to the Opera House, Jeannie made small talk. Kit looked handsome in a gray suit with a striped tie, but he was moody. She kept talking, hoping to bring back the boy who had kissed her in the Hanover elevator.

As they walked through the enormous marble lobby to find their seats, Jeannie was aware that Kit still had an uneven rolling gait. Every few steps, their shoulders bumped lightly.

"I'll always walk like a cripple," he muttered after the fifth or sixth time.

"Oh, Kit, don't say that," Jeannie pleaded. "Don't say that. Don't think it. Who except you or me would ever notice it? It's kind of distinguished, actually—like a cowboy just off his horse."

Kit snorted unappreciatively. "Distinguished, my eye! I limp like a rabbit who's been mutilated by a trap."

"Come on, Kit. Cut it out. This is my Christmas present, and we're supposed to have fun."

"We're supposed to do a lot of things," he commented as he snatched a pair of programs from the hand of a surprised usher. "But sometimes it's hard. Like now when I feel everyone's looking at me. I thought it would be different when I didn't have a crutch. But it's not. Besides, you're feeling sorry for me, and I hate that."

Jeannie walked down the aisle next to him. She did not think people were looking at him. If they were, it was probably because he and Jeannie were both so tall, not because of Kit's limp. She did not answer him.

"Do you like watching ballet?" he asked as the orchestra began to play the overture. "Even when you can't dance the way they do up on stage?"

"Yes, I do."

"Well, I don't like watching other people climb," he said, as though that was what they had been discussing in the first place.

Because the curtain was going up, there was no more time for conversation. Jeannie sank back to enjoy the lush beauty of the party scene. Despite what she had said to Kit, it distressed her to discover that Suzanne Lee, someone from her old dance class, was part of the cast. At seventeen, Suzanne was a compact girl who looked hardly older than twelve. Jeannie would not tell Kit about Suzanne.

An endless procession of dancing girls, soldiers, mice, flowers twirled before her eyes. She crossed her ankles to keep her feet from moving in time with the music. She slid her arm onto the red-velvet armrest between them, hoping Kit would do the same. He didn't. In fact, he was almost leaning away from her. His elbows were pressed tightly against his sides.

She found this distracting. She had expected that when the Opera House went dark Kit would take her hand as Mike O'Connor used to do at the movies. After a while, though, it became apparent that Kit was absorbed in his own thoughts. Then she couldn't stand it any longer. Reaching out, she took hold of his hand, squeezing it affectionately.

She could feel the tension flow from Kit's body as he laced his fingers through hers. Then he took his other hand and began to trace delicate patterns on the back of her wrist. Shivering, Jeannie sent him a quick smile. Everything was going to be all right.

It was. At intermission, Kit asked questions about classical ballet. He noticed, as she had a year before, that there were similarities between the moves of rock-climbing and dance. They stood very close to one another. Together, they smiled down on the dozens of children in party dresses and suits who were seeing the *Nutcracker* for a holiday treat.

When the performance was over, Jeannie felt so happy that she knew she would not have to force herself to give her poem to Kit. But his mood did not match hers. As soon as they headed for the car, he began to deflate as if he were a hot-air balloon with a small leak in it.

This time Jeannie did not indulge in mindless chatter. He was worrying about his mother, she decided, picturing that they would walk in to tea and find her collapsed on the kitchen floor, surrounded by empty liquor bottles.

What they did find was altogether different. A smiling, well-groomed Mrs. Hayden met them at the front door. She was wearing a beige dress, welcoming them graciously to a house that was beige and white, with vases of yellow roses. Mr. Hayden, she said, would not be joining them because he had to be at a scout meeting. "He's always scouting somewhere," she informed them with a small gesture of resignation. "But Eleanor—who's home on vacation—will take tea with us."

Jeannie was not thrilled. She was even less pleased when she and Kit walked into the living room.

"Hello," Eleanor said. "Hello, there. My goodness, I'd forgotten how tall you are."

Before Jeannie could decide how to respond, Kit did it for her. "My goodness," he said, mimicking his sister's tone, "I'd forgotten how small you are."

That exchange set the tone for the tea. Polite inquiries about cream or lemon and the passing of cucumber sandwiches and petit fours did not smooth things over.

Kit stuffed food into his mouth without taking time to taste it. He swallowed almost without chewing. Jeannie could see that he didn't trust either his mother or his sister. He was afraid there was going to be a scene.

When Eleanor got up and wandered off, Jeannie relaxed a little. Mrs. Hayden had an animation, a look in her eyes, which reminded Jeannie of Kit at his best. Although Jeannie thought she could smell a familiar sweetness clinging to Mrs. Hayden, the woman was pleasant and self-contained. She asked about the ballet. She, too, had danced as a girl, she told them.

She poured them each a second cup of tea. "I take mine with milk," she commented, "as the English do."

Kit groaned. "Mother! Jeannie doesn't care how the English drink their tea."

Mrs. Hayden looked over at Kit. "Nibbled to death by rabbits," she said. "And if you keep kicking at stones, you're going to break your toe."

"What does that mean?" he grumbled.

"You know very well what it means. It means take it easy."

Kit scowled, and Mrs. Hayden made rattling noises with her teacup. Jeannie wondered whether the two of them were about to get into an argument.

She stood up. "I think I ought to be getting home now," she said. "I've had a good time. Thank you for inviting me."

Kit seemed enormously relieved. He jumped up and put a hand on her arm. The next thing Jeannie knew, they were walking down the front path toward the car.

"I like your mother," she said.

But the words were hardly out of her mouth before she

heard a crashing sound coming from within the house. It was the sound of breaking china.

"Oh, God," Kit muttered.

"Shouldn't we go back and help?" Jeannie said.

"No, no—absolutely not. Let Eleanor help for once. Come on, let's go."

As he drove to her house, his knuckles were white against the steering wheel. Once there, he pulled up so abruptly that the tires screeched.

"Goodbye," he said tersely.

"What does that mean?"

"Don't get mixed up with me, Jeannie. That's what it means." He continued to grip the wheel. "I'm a freak from a family of freaks. Why should you give a damn about me, anyway? I was tested early. Well, maybe it was too early, and I flunked. Now—goodbye."

Jeannie slumped back against the seat. She slipped her hand into the pocket of her dress. Her fingers slid nervously over the folded wedge that was her poem. She wasn't sure she still wanted to offer it to him. Thinking about this reminded her of Kit's writing, of a question she had never asked him. "Kit?"

"What?"

"Who is Yeti? Why that name? Does it mean something?"

His hands dropped into his lap. "The monster of the mountains," he said. "The freak that wanders through the cold mountains. Alone and hunting. Alone and hunted. That's Yeti. That's me. Is that the kind of person you want to be hooked up with? That kind of freak?"

"Don't," Jeannie pleaded, reaching impulsively for his hand. She wanted to touch him now as she had in the darkened Opera House. She needed to hold on to him, to be held. Leaning forward, she rubbed her nose gently against his. Then, feeling suddenly shyer, she drew back.

Kit's hand was limp and unresponsive. "Did you do things like this with O'Connor?" he asked harshly. It was too dark to see his face, but the tone of his voice was clear. "First O'Connor, and now it's my turn. I'm always second-best. Always playing catch-up. Because of the polio. Always on the outside looking in, running to catch up to everyone else. And I hate it. Hate it."

Jeannie did not know how to answer him, but he did not wait to hear what she would say.

"Sometimes, Jeannie, I'm stupid enough to think things could be different. And they're not. You don't dance, like I don't climb. I show you Yeti, tell you personal things. But you never open up. You won't really talk, won't show me what you write. Then you pat my hand, and all I see in your eyes is pity. I hate pity."

"But I don't pity you!"

"I know pity when I see it. So get out. Goodbye. Have a good life. I loathe being pitied. And stop looking at me that way."

Jeannie pulled her hand away and stuffed it back into her pocket. "You can't see anything in this dark car. You're saying dumb, stupid things. You don't give me—or anyone—a chance."

"Shut up."

"Don't talk to me that way! I thought that you cared, that we were . . . special."

"You thought wrong," Kit told her.

"Wrong, huh? No wonder your mother says you're going to break a toe. Kicking at stones *is* what you do. All the time."

"Are you finished?"

"Yes, I'm finished, Kit. All finished. So—goodbye!"

Without giving him time to reply, she reached over and jerked the door open. "Oh, yes, and thank you for the very nice time," she said in a voice tinged with irony.

A lump was swelling in the back of her throat. She was not going to take any more punishment.

Once out of the car, she slammed the door behind her. She did not look back. As she strode toward her front door, she yanked the folded poem from her pocket. Then, methodically, she began to tear it to shreds.

Spring 1959

16

$\mathcal{A}$ RUBY-THROATED hummingbird poised in midair above Jeannie's shoulder. Then it skittered toward a plum tree blooming in the February sun. As Jeannie squinted, it dipped, spun, and angled upward until it disappeared in a cloud of pink blossoms.

Something about the blossoms, about living in California, where spring came early, created a flurry of words inside her head. *Spring, autumn. Unfurling . . . translucent . . . sunlight.* Mentally, she arranged and rearranged them. *Unfurling.* Yes, that was it. She pictured them on her tablet.

> *Out west,*
> *autumn lasts*
> *until the first buds of spring*
> *unfurl translucent petals*
> *in February sunlight . . .*

"Jeannie!" Lisabeth called impatiently. "Are you in a trance? Wake up. I think he's coming."

He was a handsome senator from the state of Massachusetts who wanted to be President. His name was John Kennedy, and he was campaigning on the West Coast. One of his aides had promised that he would make a brief stop at a noontime rally organized by the Young Democrats Club of Jackson High. It was a public rally being held in the plaza of the small park across from the school.

Lisabeth was there because she wanted to gather material for the lead article in the next issue of the *Banner*. Jeannie had accompanied her because she wanted to be outside on a day that smelled as if spring had truly arrived.

> *in February sunlight . . .*
> *perhaps before that last red leaf*
> *lofts into the wind—*

"Come on, Jeannie, you're no company at all when you get that way. I thought you were excited about seeing him."

Jeannie would have to finish her poem later. Besides, she *was* looking forward to seeing John Kennedy. This was her last semester in high school, and any diversion was welcome. She was ready to leave, ready to move across the Bay to Berkeley, where she would be going to college in the fall.

"Cabin fever," was her father's diagnosis. "Senior sickness." She felt as if everything she was doing at school—except anatomy—was a repeat of something she had done before.

No fever or sickness had infected Lisabeth. Her enthusiasm never flagged. "He's special. Young, handsome —and he's going to be President!"

Jeannie looked down at her friend. "Without you," she remarked companionably, "I don't know how I'd be making it through this year."

Lisabeth shrugged and wrinkled up her nose. "Silly— you don't mean that and you—hey, look over there. There's Kit. I can't—just can't—understand why you dumped him."

Jeannie didn't answer, but she did turn in Kit's direction. Seeing him was no surprise. She knew he would be there. His group—the Birdmen—were playing at the rally. The Birdmen had formed a jazz quartet. Kit, who had taken up photography and magic with ease, was developing into a drummer to accompany friends who played piano, saxophone, and bass. Dmitri was the group's manager.

She and Kit hadn't spoken in over a year. On a campus with three thousand students, it was not hard to avoid someone. Although she didn't know if Kit's surgery had been a success, it would have been hard not to know something about the Birdmen. They were unique. A small select group interested in jazz, rock climbing, and —more recently—in grass-roots politics.

Jeannie's body responded to their music, to the smooth rhythms coming over the P.A. system. Swaying gently, she examined Kit. He looked older. Still, not too much older, not too much different. As she stared at him, she felt sad.

This year she had gone out with Mike O'Connor, who was now a freshman at nearby U.S.F., and with a quiet, soft-spoken boy named Russell. She was friendly with both of them, but not close. Only Kit had ever stirred deep feelings inside of her. Yet the two of them had never been able to get along without arguing.

Lisabeth's voice rambled on, interrupting Jeannie's maze of thoughts about Kit. "Everyone's getting restless. The music's gone on much too long. He was supposed to be here by now."

Lisabeth was right. A large and unsettled crowd pressed in around them. It included many people who were not students, because the morning paper had an article on the rally for the senator. Voices were beginning to chant "We want Kennedy. We want Kennedy!"

As the chanting grew louder, Jeannie saw Kit leave his drums and disappear from the platform. Although the other three kept playing, the noise from the spectators increased, until it was so loud that the music piped over the P.A. system was almost drowned out.

"Something's gone wrong," Lisabeth shouted into Jeannie's ear.

Jeannie nodded in agreement. "I think I'm going to leave," she told Lisabeth.

"Why?"

"I don't like this. I feel like I can't get enough air."

Lisabeth grabbed at her arm. "Stay, please. Look, Kit's back, and he's got Silverlake with him."

Jeremy Silverlake was the principal of Jackson High, a barrel-chested, balding former coach. He was well liked and known for his booming voice. Though he never used a megaphone, he always gave the impression he was using one.

Silverlake picked up the microphone. Holding it as if it were a football about to be passed off to a receiver, he aimed his words at the now-angry crowd.

John Kennedy was not coming, he informed them. There had been a misunderstanding, a missed plane. The senator would not be at their rally. The crowd booed and yelled.

"Don't be poor sports," he urged. "It isn't whether you win or lose, but how you play the game. Now, young Jack Kennedy plays ball, and he would want you to be *good* sports. Don't go on the offense over something understandable. *Defense* is the name of the game."

Jeannie glanced from Silverlake to Kit. Kit had a funny half grin on his face. A rather self-satisfied grin, she thought. Bringing the principal-coach to speak to the crowd was going to work. She began to laugh. From other parts of the crowd, occasional chuckles and giggles were surfacing.

The principal gripped the mike even tighter and continued with his oration. *"Defense.* Defense—I've always said—is the key to life. A person who understands defense and the good of the team is an unselfish, sharing person. And young Jack Kennedy has been a team player all his life. So if you're a Republican and can't stand the guy, or if you're a Democrat and want to be part of the team that wants to elect him President, remember *defense.* Forget offensive moves for now. Back off. Accept mistakes."

His words were sincere, yet at the same time they were ridiculous. But he had started something which he seemed determined to finish.

"So Jack Kennedy isn't here. You're here. If you're truly loyal, you won't give up because someone on his staff loused things up. Be good sports, be good teammates, and disperse quietly. Because J.F.K. doesn't want a bunch of self-important poor sports on his team. If you're for Jack, on Jack's team, you'll march away from here with shoulders back and heads held high."

By now Jeannie and Lisabeth were holding on to one another, rocking with laughter. They were not alone, either. The crowd's mood had turned from ugliness to hilarity. Apparently satisfied, Silverlake stepped away from the mike. The students and other spectators obeyed his advice. In small groups, laughing, they began to leave.

"Have you ever," Lisabeth gasped, "heard anything in your life like that? How do I put *that* into a story?"

"Just stick to the facts, ma'am," Jeannie advised. "No one would believe quotes from that speech." Even as she answered, she wondered if Silverlake had given that speech in earnest or if he had decided to be a buffoon, a parody of himself, as a way to head off trouble.

As her laughter trailed away, Jeannie realized that she still had her eyes fastened on Kit. Looking at him reminded her suddenly of the plum tree blooming on the plaza, of the unfinished poem inside her head.

It had a beginning, a middle, and effortlessly—unfurling—an end. *Unfurling.*

> *Out west,*
> *autumn lasts*
> *until the first buds of spring*
> *unfurl translucent petals*
> *in February sunlight.*
> *Perhaps before that last red leaf*
> *lofts into the wind,*
> *you and I should try unfurling*
> *some of the tight hidden thoughts*
> *held*
> *alone*
> *among our roots.*

Her eyes were watering. She swiped at them with the back of one hand. Then, without taking time to explain anything to Lisabeth, she started up toward the platform where Kit was standing. Before he disappeared into the crowd, she wanted to see him.

She was about to mount the steps when something caught her attention. A disheveled young woman dressed all in black. Clinging to her skirt was an exceptionally dirty-looking child.

The woman seemed to be dancing in the center of the plaza. For a moment, Jeannie stared at her. The woman was not very different from herself in age or in dress. Jeannie had taken to dressing in black, feeling that it suited her as a writer, as an outsider.

While Jeannie watched, the young woman's dance suddenly became a drunken reel. Then, a moment later, she collapsed onto the cement and lay there without moving. Instinctively, Jeannie rushed forward.

"Stand back," she told the few remaining people. "Stand back and give her air."

As Jeannie was speaking, the child threw himself on the cement beside his mother and began to cry. Jeannie didn't have time to deal with him. She had to do something for the unconscious woman.

"Dirty beatnik," someone commented. "She's probably bombed or spaced out. On drugs or Gallo."

Jeannie did not look up. She felt the woman's forehead, pulled back her eyelids, checked her breathing.

"Move her across the street into the school," someone suggested.

The child continued to cry. He kicked at the ground, at his mother, at Jeannie.

"Don't move her!" Jeannie said. "Call an ambulance—immediately." The child kicked her in the ribs. "Oof—won't someone do something about *him?*"

"I will," answered a familiar voice from behind.

It was Kit. Kit would help. He would manage the boy and the onlookers, so she could do something.

The woman's pulse was irregular, slow. Her breathing was shallow. Her face was drained of all color.

"Check her purse for drugs," a man said.

That was a good suggestion, and Jeannie took it. When she opened the woman's pouchlike purse, she found little bottles of insulin and hypodermic needles. One of the bottles was empty. One of the needles had been used.

The woman, Jeannie concluded, might have taken an overdose of insulin. At the hospital, Jeannie had worked with enough diabetic children to know about overdoses of insulin.

Kit, having hushed the boy, was bouncing him in his arms. "What do you do for an overdose?" he asked, indicating that he had grasped the situation as rapidly as Jeannie.

"Sugar."

"Well, then, I think you should *do* something before she gets worse. Someone here must have juice or a Coke we can pour down her throat."

Jeannie shook her head. "I can't take that responsibility. Maybe she needs *more* insulin instead of less. I'm no doctor . . ."

"But you know about these procedures. You work in a hospital."

Jeannie shook her head. "I don't. Haven't for months. And I'm *not* a doctor."

Silverlake was standing next to Kit. "Wait for the ambulance," he advised. "I can hear the sirens."

Jeannie nodded in agreement. She would tell the attendants that the woman was a diabetic. Then they could take over.

Only a few minutes later, the ambulance doors closed and Jeannie found herself inside with two attendants, a driver, an unconscious patient, a dirty child, and Kit. They were going to Mission Emergency Hospital. Kit had suggested that the two of them could look after the child until some relative was found.

As they sped across San Francisco with red lights flashing and sirens wailing, Jeannie looked over at Kit. They were perched on hard wooden seats across from one another, jolting up and down with the bumps in the street. The child in Kit's arms was drifting off to sleep.

"Kit," she said, letting his name substitute for a dozen other things she couldn't manage to say. All of a sudden, it was as if no time had passed—as if the ballet had been only a day before. *Unfurling . . . tight hidden thoughts . . . alone.* "Kit."

He raised an eyebrow at her, responding more to the

tone of her voice than to his name. "All dressed in black. You look like a licorice stick."

She laughed softly. "I like black. But why is it—why do you always think I look like some kind of candy?"

Kit answered her question with a question. "Have you noticed that we always seem to be going to hospitals together? We've got to stop meeting like this."

"Why candy?" Jeannie asked, persistent enough to ignore his joking. She was warm, yet at the same time she was shivering. "Used to be a peppermint. Now licorice. How come?"

Kit grinned. "That's for you to figure out." Shifting the boy from one shoulder to the other, he changed the subject. "Still writing poetry?"

. . . you and I should try unfurling . . . tight hidden thoughts . . . Jeannie nodded . . . *held alone . . . among our roots . . .* "Yes," she said.

"Seems like that was what our last argument was about. When I behaved like a rhino charging at a riverboat."

Jeannie twisted her fingers together in her lap. "I'm out of practice—but I think *I* was a little like a groundhog who had just seen his shadow."

Kit's eyes were laughing. They did not look fierce or angry. They were trying to tell her something about why he always compared her to candies.

Embarrassed, she looked down. It was then she realized, for the first time, that Kit wore no brace, carried no crutch or cane. Sitting across from her, he looked like any high-school senior who had never had polio. As if he were reading her mind, he freed one hand and pulled up the leg of his jeans. "Everything works. This leg's a little shorter and—well, you can see."

She saw. She was looking at a left ankle which was still only half normal size. But Kit said it worked, and to him, that was obviously what mattered.

Hesitantly, she looked up. "Mmm . . . Kit," she said, feeling as tentative as her fourteen-year-old self had been, "could we—could we try again?"

Instead of answering, he frowned. "I never realize," he told her, "how alone I feel most of the time until I'm with you and I don't feel alone. Does that make sense? Do you know what I mean?"

It made sense. She knew what he meant. His admission was part of the *unfurling of translucent petals.* She wanted, needed the same closeness he did. No one she had ever known had affected her as strongly as Kit. She wanted to reach out and hold him. But they were jolting along in an ambulance. In Kit's arms was a sick woman's child. Moaning, that woman was beginning to regain consciousness.

"Oh, Jeannie," Kit said, ". . . Jeannie West. Jeannie with the light-brown hair. Will you laugh—you won't, will you—if I tell you that Yeti has missed you?"

17

JEANNIE followed Kit down the face of the cliff. It was the only way, he told her, to get from Devil's Slide to the little beach below. Listening to his instructions, she clung to the rock. She could hear the ocean, but she did not try to measure how far she was above the water.

As they climbed, Jeannie remembered a long-ago morning near Twin Peak. Today, however, things were different. Kit's left leg was dependable now. It had a set of muscles that worked. The only thing that was the same was the way she was shaking. While her head told her she was not frightened, her body sent out distress signals.

By telling herself that the cliff was not dangerous and that there was soft sand at the bottom, she was able to continue. The rock was crumbly, but it had safe niches for her hands and feet. And Kit, with patience, helped guide every move she made. At last, she saw the beach. As she gave a sigh of relief, Kit let go and slid the last ten feet.

He raised his voice over the sound of the waves and called to her. "Push out from that ledge like I did and slide. I'll catch you."

Jeannie, trying to ignore her fear, pushed and let go. For one long moment she was unprotected. Then Kit's arms took hold of her, broke her fall. Together, they tumbled backward into the damp sand.

"That leg," Kit groaned. "Climbing's all right, but—when I just stand—my balance is lousy."

Jeannie did not mind the dampness or the fact that they had fallen, because Kit still had hold of her. They were lying side by side on the beach, and for once they were completely alone. On impulse, Jeannie did what she had not done in the ambulance a week before. Shifting her position, she wrapped her arms around his neck. She drew her face close to Kit's. The kiss they exchanged was gentle and only slightly sandy.

After a long moment, they let go of one another and pulled back. Rolling over, they arranged themselves so that they were on their stomachs face to face. When Jeannie propped herself up on her elbows, Kit did the same.

"I don't think," she told him, "I've ever been kissed in the daytime. Only at night—in someone's car."

"Been kissed," Kit snorted. "I know you've been kissed in an elevator—in the daytime. And as for now, were you *being* kissed? I thought you were the one doing the kissing."

Jeannie reached out and pulled at his nose. "Mmm . . . well, I may have started it, but . . ."

Kit nodded. "So—okay, it was both of us."

Then, without discussion, they began to shape a castle in the wet sand. They dug, scooped, and piled mounds of sand until they had constructed a turreted castle with its own moat.

From time to time their hands touched companionably, but their motions were slow and relaxed. Although Jeannie thought about the yellow tablet hidden in the knapsack strapped to her shoulders, there was no hurry to pull it out and show it to Kit. The sun was shining. The sound of breakers was soothing. Later he would see some of her work.

After a while, Jeannie broke the silence. "I hope we've

built it far enough back," she mused, "so the tide won't eat it."

"Now that's a real difference between us," Kit said, digging into the moat until a pool of water appeared. "You expect things to last. And I'm always afraid to. I see things you don't."

"Like what?"

"Like this is a tidal beach, Jeannie. That's why it's so wet. When the tide comes in, there's no beach. Look at the waterline on the cliff."

As Jeannie was mourning the impending destruction of their castle, Kit offered up a piece of unsolicited information. "I had a girl friend last summer. At the camp where I worked—a camp for handicapped children. Her name was Maureen."

"What was she like?" Jeannie asked.

Kit grinned. "Oh, like a duck—friendly, nosy—she followed me around quacking."

"Come on, Kit."

"No, no, I speak the truth. But you, Jeannie West, you're a long-necked swan, and I've never known anyone like you . . ."

Jeannie picked up a seagull feather lying in the sand, a feather that might have triggered Kit's bird images. She stuck it in the sandy turret, feeling a small stab of jealousy over a girl who had followed Kit around.

Kit spoke again. "Tell me something."

"What?"

Kit squinted. "Do you believe in fate?"

"Never thought about it."

"Well, I have. A lot. I mean, was it fate that I should get polio just before everyone else was going to get vaccine? Fate that I should want to climb mountains instead of play chess? That we met because I was in the hospital and you think you're going to be a doctor?"

Rolling over on her back, Jeannie stared up at the blank blue sky. "I'm not going to be a doctor," she said.

"But last week—with that woman—you were wonderful."

"Maybe," she admitted. "But things that seemed simple when I was Jill's age look opaque. Like a crystal ball that's filled with mist." Inside her head, a handful of words stirred. The sky was hypnotizing her, so that she hardly realized that she was speaking the words out loud. "... *a paperweight with a wet snowstorm ... a crystal ball cooled by a cloud ...*"

Suddenly Kit pulled himself to a sitting position. "Did you bring them?" he asked.

"The poems?" She nodded. "Some. Yes."

"Can I see them?"

They had argued about this before, but now she was writing more poetry, better poetry.

"Yes," she told him. Then she asked a delaying question. "Do you still write?"

A pen was clipped to the pocket of his shirt. He pulled it out and rolled it between his fingers. "Not much. Too busy with schoolwork, the Birdmen, climbing. Which reminds me—you still dance?"

They did have a lot to catch up on. "Dance Club at school? No, I stopped. But I'm starting again. A new class down on Market Street—jazz ballet. Flo, my teacher, is terrific."

"She doesn't think you're too tall?"

Laughing, Jeannie shaded her eyes to see if Kit was teasing her. He wasn't. "No, Flo says tall dancers project force and power."

Kit stood up. He reached down and pulled her to her feet. "Come on," he urged, "let's climb onto the rocks. Before the tide comes in. We can read your stuff out there."

Jeannie didn't mind. It provided one more convenient delay as they made their way along the dark, slippery rocks to a point where the ocean almost completely surrounded them. Kit was slightly ahead. She examined the small brace visible below his hiking shorts. It went from the knee and was anchored to his boot. It was meant for climbing—to protect the thin left ankle from getting broken. Otherwise, Kit looked and moved like anyone else.

Once out on the point, they seated themselves in a curved piece of rock as though they were riding between the twin humps of a camel. Jeannie was in front, Kit behind as they stared at the waves washing over a forest of tiny sea palms.

In a cold tropic forest of sea palms . . . "Why don't you write? What are you going to do?" Jeannie asked as her words reminded her again of his.

"I don't know. Things look misty. Like your *crystal ball cooled by a cloud*. Except for college. And climbing."

"Where?" Jeannie asked, feeling relaxed, comfortable.

"Half Dome this summer. Or, if I'm not good enough for that—Royal Arches."

"Isn't that going to be dangerous?"

"I think I can do Royal Arches," he told her, as a hardness she remembered crept into his voice.

She did not want to hear any more about climbing. Her uncle had said Kit would never climb. "What about college? Where?"

"Harvard, I hope. If I get in. If I get a job to help pay my way."

"What's wrong with Berkeley? With California?"

"Nothing, but it's not far enough from my mother, from my father. Three thousand miles seems like about the right distance, even if the mountains aren't nearly as good."

155

"Always the mountains," Jeannie mused.

"Maybe *you* should come East to school," he said, sending a puff of warm breath into her hair. "Then we could see each other, be together, like now. Instead of being alone. I think it's left from being sick—that sense of being so alone . . ."

Jeannie leaned back slightly, pressing her gray-black sweatshirt against Kit's shoulder, letting her hand rest on his cheek. "But I've never been sick. And I still feel that way."

"Alone?" Kit pulled at a lock of her hair. "You do? With me? Still alone?"

"Less," she admitted. "Though I've never figured out why."

"Do you have to?"

She shook her head. "I guess not. But maybe it has something to do with loving . . ."

Kit did not answer. Nor did she continue. She didn't know that she loved Kit. She wasn't sure why she had suggested it. As always, she was drawn to him yet at the same time pulled away. She was puzzled, uncertain. She wondered whether things would be clearer if she and Kit kissed again. He made no move, though, and she was not willing to be once more accused of kissing him.

After a long silence, Kit reminded her that she had promised to show him her tablet. Slowly, she bent forward and pulled it from the knapsack resting between her knees. Then, as she opened it, he peered over her shoulder, reading the poem that was written on the first page.

Gossamer
like the shimmering stitches
of a spider's web. No promises,

1 5 6

nothing but this moment's
fragile beauty
showing off its intricacy
in glinting sunlight.

Break the web if you will. It's
not meant to wound, to trap
or to bind
only to remind
how gossamer are the shuttled threads
spun from one to one.

Before Jeannie knew what was happening, Kit whipped his pen from his pocket and was using it to make marks on her tablet. Suddenly, "shimmering," "fragile," and "glinting" all had circles around them. His ink had invaded her pale penciled page.

"Too many adjectives," he said. "And you ought to sign your name when you finish a poem."

He had spoiled her poem with his ink and his comments. Without attempting to explain, she shoved the tablet into the dark safety of her knapsack.

"Oh, God," Kit moaned, sticking his pen back in his pocket. "Did I really do that? I didn't mean to. I'm sorry. Hey, Jeannie—I really am sorry."

"It's okay." What had happened had been her fault as well as his. She did not want to argue, but she knew it would be a while before she showed him her poetry again.

They were both still struggling to recover when Kit pointed down at the beach. "Look. The tide's coming in. We've got to get out of here."

A few minutes later, when they reached the base of the cliff, the incoming waves were already rolling in against its walls. Their castle was a lump of sand.

"This way. You first," Kit said, gesturing.

Jeannie looked up. There was no visible path. "I'd better follow," she said.

"You can't. We won't make it unless I boost you. We *slid* the last ten feet, remember?"

Belatedly, she remembered. She was unwilling, however, to lead the way up the looming cliff to the highway, where the car was parked.

"Please go," Kit urged. "Now. This beach is being washed away from under our feet."

As if to illustrate his words, a wave crested, drenching them. Jeannie shivered.

"Go," Kit commanded, using the non-negotiable pick-up-my-pencil voice she knew so well.

She obeyed. When he boosted her, she grabbed at the ledge and pulled herself up onto it. As they stood there, looking down, something occurred to her.

"Kit? How are you going to get up?"

He had a sheepish expression on his face. "I'm not sure."

"But you've been here before. Down and up."

He shook his head. "No. Never. But don't panic. Rocks and panic don't mix."

Jeannie didn't say another word. Kneeling, she watched as he scrambled for the rock ledge. By getting a running start, he hoped to grasp enough of the rock to pull himself to the ledge. He tried it once, then again and again. Each time, he slipped and fell backward into the wet sand.

He was determined, angry, and he didn't like looking foolish in front of her. He wasn't going to make it, though. She commanded herself to stay calm until she found a solution to the situation. At last, it came to her.

As she had done earlier in the day, she pushed out and back and slid the ten feet to the beach.

"Why did you do that?" Kit yelled.

She ignored both the incoming waves and his tone of voice. They were going to try her method. "I'll boost *you*," she said, "and when you're on the ledge, you'll be strong enough to grab my hands and help pull me."

Jeannie's idea worked. Fifteen or twenty minutes later, they were at the top of the cliff, looking down at the tiny crescent of wet beach they had just escaped from.

She was so relieved to be safely back by the car that she didn't protest as Kit wrapped his arms around her from behind. His pen was once again out of his pocket and in his hand. He wrote something in the palm of her right hand.

"How could you have taken us down not knowing how we were going to get up?" she asked, paying little attention to the pen.

"I think there's another way," he admitted. "Around that rocky point to another, larger beach with steps going up."

Jeannie wanted to break loose from his arms, but she didn't. "Have you ever gone that way?"

"No, but I'm pretty sure it can be done. Oh, Jeannie, you're so pretty. A pretty, pretty girl. Please don't get angry with me. Don't be so afraid of risks. Trust me. Will you show me your poems again if I keep my lousy pen away? Will you climb with me again?"

Jeannie reeled from his barrage of questions. If his arms hadn't been around her, she would have been shouting at him. Instead, her anger faded as his arms made her cold, wet body feel warmer.

He was right. She did not take risks. Still, he seemed to take too many. Then she looked to see what he had written on her palm.

In tiny precise letters, the ballpoint had formed a message. "Yeti loves you," it said.

Jeannie pulled loose. "Talk about not taking risks," she said, turning to face him. " 'Yeti' loves me. Yeti again? What about Kit? What about Christopher Hayden?"

"Loving is taking a really big risk," he said as she examined him, looking from the brace on his foot to the earnest half smile on his face. "But I think, Jeannie, that we are going to be seeing a lot of each other."

18

THE CAT lay in the pan with its eyes open and its dark, swollen tongue curling out from beneath its teeth. Kit threw a cloth over the head.

"If I'd known," he told Jeannie, "that you and I were going to get the one with the tongue, I would never have asked to move into your section."

They were in anatomy. The odor of formaldehyde rose from the dead animal they were dissecting.

"Are these fumes poisonous, I wonder?" Jeannie asked Kit as they uncoiled the cat's amazingly long small intestine.

Kit stood next to her, his shoulder bumping affectionately against hers. The two of them had never taken a lab together before, and she was enjoying it.

"Poisonous!" he exclaimed, letting loops of intestine droop over the scalpel in his hand. "I don't know how it will affect us, but look what it's done to Chaplin."

Chaplin was the name of their dead cat. He had gotten his name because of the comical look the terrible tongue gave to his black-and-white face. Although Chaplin had been covered with black-and-white fur, most of it had been discarded in the dissecting process. Now the dismal animal was furred only on his face and feet.

"At least we know he won't catch cold," Jeannie whispered ghoulishly, "because he *is* wearing his warm socks and mittens."

Kit laughed. Responding to her gallows humor with some of his own, he cut her initials from a discarded swatch of cat skin. Jeannie saw that she and Kit were not the only students joking over a carcass in a pan. Jokes of the same sort were flying all over the lab. Examining dead creatures seemed to bring out an endless array of sick humor.

As soon as Jeannie's initials were finished, someone at the next table cut Kit's from the skin of a ginger-colored cat. Then, before either of them could protest, the four initials were pinned to the bulletin board to signal that everyone in the class knew that Jeannie and Kit were going together.

Despite the low level of the humor, Jeannie found dissecting fascinating. Inside an animal, everything was magnificently well ordered. When she forgot the fumes, the sight was beautiful—an astonishing array of color, shining organs, membranes, veins, arteries.

While she was totally absorbed in dissecting, the clouds in the crystal ball shifted until she thought she was being drawn again toward the study of medicine. But at other moments her attention drifted from the cat; and picking up a pencil, she searched for some clue to what was happening to her this spring.

In her lab book, along with diagrams smudged by Chaplin's tissue, she was trying to write a poem about some of her feelings. Kit, who was more interested in Jeannie than he was in anatomy, examined the poem as she continued to explore the carcass. She had, in the last few weeks, begun to be less sensitive about allowing him to see what she wrote, but it still was not easy.

It became more difficult again when Kit decided to read her poem aloud and test its sound.

My Heart

should be ventricles, atriums
bright hot liquid coursing through
vena cava and aorta
into arterials
of rivers, streams, brooks, rills

yet it seems a dim blue ice cave
its chamber clenched about
a mammoth calf that bleats
in melting tones

Flinching, Jeannie glanced around to see if any of their classmates had heard him. Apparently not. They were busy exchanging cat jokes. As Jeannie braced herself for Kit's comment, she reexamined the poem. She could not understand how it had come out on paper with such a somber tone when she was so happy. There were many things about writing, about poetry, she didn't understand. Even now, her work seemed unsatisfactory and new words were pounding in her head, demanding a place in the poem. *Network . . . ruddy . . . sluice . . . a sluicing of rivers, brooks, streams, rills . . .*

When Kit's voice broke into her thoughts, it had a comforting, reassuring tone. "Wonderful, Jeannie. This one is complex. I'm not sure what it means."

Unable to answer, she bent over and poked at Chaplin's stomach with small clippers. Kit didn't take a pen to her work any more, but his compliments were as difficult to accept as his criticism. Though she was trying to take more risks, to trust him, it was painful, frightening.

"What made you write this, Jeannie? Where did the cave come from? And that mammoth calf? I like it, but . . ."

Sometimes she felt as if she were a sculpture being

carved by Kit. She liked his attention, respected his judgment, yet something alarmed her.

"Do I influence you," she asked him, as she removed a hairball from the cat's stomach, "as much as you influence me?"

If Kit had a satisfactory answer for her, it was lost as the bell rang, indicating that the lab and school were over for the day. Their discussion was put aside as they threw a towel over the cat, washed themselves and their instruments, and hurried off.

As they walked hand in hand along the sidewalk toward his house, the topic of who was influencing whom was forgotten. They had an appointment to keep. They were expected at Kit's house for tea. Martin Storey was to be there, too.

"What do you think my mother has up her sleeve?" Kit mused.

"I thought this was for fun. Because Martin's your doctor and was so good to you while you were sick."

Turning slightly, Kit rubbed his nose against her ear. "Nothing my mother does is just for fun. Everything has its use and purpose. Even drinking, I suppose. Helps her with difficult things. Like me. Like my father . . ."

Jeannie thought for a moment. "Hmm . . . well, Uncle Martin doesn't do many things for fun, either." She stopped walking. "I bet they *are* plotting. Why didn't we figure that out before?"

Kit pulled at her, making her move forward again. "C'mon. This is a command performance. Unless, of course, you think we can bow out. I could call Dmitri and the three of us could go climbing."

He was teasing her. "Between the devil and the deep blue sea," she mumured, letting him lead her on toward his house.

Martin and Mrs. Hayden were waiting in the living

room when they arrived. As always, Kit's mother was impeccably dressed. Today she was in navy, with a white carnation pinned to the collar of her dress. Martin would have looked handsome if he hadn't just begun to grow a moustache. He had some notion that a moustache was going to make him look older.

Jeannie did not feel impeccable. She felt distinctly peccable in a black leotard with a wrinkled black-and-brown batik skirt wrapped around her waist.

"Oh, gosh," she told Mrs. Hayden apologetically, "I should have dressed up. And, well—we still smell from formaldehyde, I think."

"Nonsense," Kit's mother said. "You're perfect. But if you're worried about the lab smells, let's go see if lemon juice will take care of them."

Then she whisked Jeannie off to the kitchen, where she produced cut lemons to squeeze over her hands and arms. Kit declined to be bothered.

Every time Jeannie went into that kitchen, she imagined that some cabinet would fly open, revealing caches of empty liquor bottles. Yet this never happened. Nor did she ever see any evidence that drinking affected the woman. In front of Jeannie, Mrs. Hayden was always calm and self-contained. Kit's fear revolved around the unexpected, the fear of having her out of control in public. If Jeannie had not once witnessed such a moment, she might have thought Kit was imagining things. Only Mrs. Hayden's breath served as a reminder of her use of liquor.

"There now," the woman said, claiming Jeannie's attention again. "A lick and a promise and we've taken care of the problem. But—one more thing . . ."

"What?" Jeannie asked.

"If I have never said it, I like you, young woman. You seem to be a person of real substance."

Jeannie flushed. She didn't know how to respond. Mrs.

Hayden didn't seem to be expecting any answer, because she went on speaking. "It is my opinion that you are good for Kit. Stabilizing. But I do wish one thing . . ."

"Anything," Jeannie offered. "I'm happy to help."

"The climbing," his mother said, dropping her voice to a whisper. "He must give it up. It's too dangerous. Not wise, especially with a weak leg. Don't answer me now, dear. But if you can help, I would appreciate it." Mrs. Hayden raised her chin in the air. "Well, now, let's go have our tea."

So, Kit had been right to say his mother had some motive behind asking them for tea. Once again, Jeannie found herself in the position of being asked to persuade Kit to do something. And she did not like it. She did not like the idea of being Kit's keeper. Rock climbing, however, did not prove to be the only subject on the agenda. As soon as tea had been poured, Martin Storey brought up another subject.

"I'm thinking of opening a new rehab unit at the hospital," he said, spooning liberal amounts of sugar into his cup. "And I need some intelligent, understanding young people to make it fly this summer."

"What kind of rehab unit?" Kit asked in a decidedly suspicious tone.

"For young people—children with various physical disabilities. Some post-polios, some accident victims. I'm envisioning a relaxing place where people can sit and exchange meaningful information."

Martin Storey was back in medical school studying psychiatry. He had finished his work with newborns and moved on to a newer interest.

One of the things that Jeannie loved best about her uncle was the fact that if he wasn't pleased with what he was doing, he moved on. If his crystal ball was cloudy, he created a wind to clear the air so he could read a new fortune. Kit was like that, too. She wondered if she would ever be that way.

She liked Martin's idea. "Maybe Jill would help. I was working at Hanover at her age. And what about Trilby?" she continued, thinking out loud. "I still write to her sometimes. Maybe she could come down from Shasta."

When she glanced over at Kit, she saw that his mouth was tight-lipped as it always was if any discussion revolved around handicaps or hospitals. "What happened to the babies?" he asked with almost no veneer of politeness.

Martin was more than his equal. "They didn't seem to have enough to say," he commented, "so I decided I had best return my efforts to smart-mouthed youngsters."

Temporarily silenced, Kit stood up and slouched over to the corner that held his drums. Seating himself on a stool, he picked up a pair of sticks and began to tap lightly on one of them.

"Talk to Jeannie," he advised, "if you need a nurse-maid. Get Jill and Trilby to tag along after her. But I'm going to be in Yosemite, climbing."

Mrs. Hayden sent a pleading look in Jeannie's direction. Jeannie took a large bite of peanut-butter cookie so she would not have to say anything to anyone. Afternoon tea had been a setup to convince him to give up climbing. She felt like a deer in a forest fire who couldn't decide which way to run.

"Actually," Kit continued, when he saw that he had silenced everyone, "Jeannie would be a swell choice. Why, considering the way she's digging into our cat in anatomy class, she'd be perfect for the job. She could slice right into those kids' brains and diagnose their problems."

"Are you going to shunt aside my suggestion without even considering it?" Martin asked Kit.

"Speak to Jeannie—speak to her. She's the one who wields the wicked scalpel."

Jeannie saw that she was being forced to choose sides and indicate where her loyalty lay. It was, she found, surprisingly easy to do.

"Well," she began, imitating Kit's mocking tone, "Chaplin—our anatomy cat—is only a beginning. I have this strange urge to try my skill on something larger. After I figure out, of course, what that gruesome brown peanut-buttery stuff is curdled around the kidneys. Oh, excuse me, Uncle Martin, you are eating one of those crumbly cookies now, aren't you?"

Laughing, Martin reached for another cookie. He was not going to let Jeannie and Kit beat him that easily. Jeannie wasn't brave enough to look over at Mrs. Hayden. At this moment, Jeannie understood how having a son like Kit and a husband in love with the Boy Scouts could put a serious strain on her.

"Maybe," Kit suggested, "we could drape Chaplin's innards like streamers around the room." His words were accompanied by a light marching rhythm on the drums.

Jeannie considered his idea for a moment, then offered an unpalatable one of her own. "Or mount his head on a plaque, like our mascot . . . and with that—"

". . . tongue, that awful lolling tongue, Jeannie. Oh, the kids should love him!"

"I am not in need of any immediate answer," Martin said, speaking as if she and Kit were not being unforgivably rude. "But what I did have in mind would be rather more like a clubroom than an operating theater with spare parts strewn about."

"Well, then," Kit advised, standing up and moving to the center of the room, "what you need is a soda jerk. And I'm the wrong jerk."

"Think about it," Martin said.

"I don't need to think. What I want to do is climb. And you, Jeannie? You'll climb with me, won't you?

How about next week at Pinnacles? It will help get me ready for Yosemite." Then, turning, he headed into the kitchen.

As soon as Kit left, Jeannie's manners returned. Contrite, she offered to pour more tea. She told Martin and Mrs. Hayden that, even if she decided not to help, the program sounded like a good idea. Jeannie kept peering toward the kitchen, hoping to catch a glimpse of Kit. When he did not come back, she began to wonder what he was doing. Finally, she excused herself and headed off to find him.

But he was not there. The back door hung open to indicate the direction in which he had fled. Like a string of his own silk scarves, he had vanished.

19

*J*EANNIE pulled on her old clothes and began to lace up the hiking boots Kit had borrowed for her. Jill sat on the bed watching.

"They're so ugly, Jeannie. Really ugly. Make your feet look like gunboats. Are you really going to do this dumb thing?"

Concentrating on crisscrossing the laces, Jeannie did not bother to answer. The dumb thing Jill had referred to was an expedition of sorts—one with ropes and pitons. Because she was angry that Mrs. Hayden and Martin tried to persuade Kit to give up his summer plans, Jeannie had agreed to climb with him. Now she was determined to go through with it.

Her parents trusted Kit. They did not seem disturbed that their daughter would be perched on a cliff, protected only by a piece of rope. Jeannie's mother offered them an early pancake breakfast so they would eat well before they went. Her father's only advice was to be careful on the road because "haste makes waste."

Their complacency, Jeannie realized, was a reflection of the fact that they had never seen anything but the polite, intellectual side of Kit. They didn't know about the wild streak that made him do things like take her down to isolated beaches without knowing how they would get back up.

Today, with Dmitri, they were going south of San

Francisco to a place called Pinnacles. It was the eroded remains of an extinct volcano, a place known for its excellent short climbs.

"Aren't you afraid?" Jill asked. "Can he really climb with that leg?"

Refusing to admit to any of her qualms, Jeannie grabbed for her faded black sweatshirt. "See you later," she said.

As she sat next to Kit in the car on the way to Pinnacles, Jeannie scribbled a crude poem on her tablet. She reworked it once, then once again. She could have talked with Kit about the way she felt because Dmitri was asleep in the back seat, but she didn't. Every time she tried to discuss something with Kit, she ended up wrong or on the defensive. He always seemed to be right.

When they arrived, Kit stopped the car. Dmitri sat up. He stretched. Then, without saying anything, he got out of the car and closed the door behind him.

Kit turned to Jeannie. Leaning over, he gazed down at the tablet and began to read her poem.

> *Fear screeches through my middle ear*
> *like fingernails across a blackboard,*
> *destroying balance, playing an off-key tune*
> *that makes me dance with a marionette's*
> *jerky, stumbling steps.*
>
> *Yet because*
> *I trust him, I shall let him lead*
> *and banish paralyzing terror*
> *by pressing his nails into my palm.*
> *J-M.W.*

As Kit finished reading, he took her hand and pressed his nails into the palm of her left hand.

"Thank you," she whispered.

"You're welcome," he whispered back. "Your work is getting good, Jeannie, really good. Deep—close to the bone."

Something about the compliment disturbed her. It was again the voice of a teacher speaking to a favorite pupil. As she reread her poem, it bothered her, too. It had a lot of Yeti qualities; it exposed too much.

Suddenly uneasy, she opened the car door and called out to Dmitri. "Well, good morning. I guess it's time to wake up and give the beginner a lesson."

Lessons, she quickly discovered, began not with climbing but with equipment. Before Kit and Dmitri would take her anywhere near rock, they had to check out their gear item by item. They explained bowlines and belays, carabiners, rappelling. They examined ropes, slings, pitons. Only when all this information, in its own strange language, had been satisfactorily imparted were they prepared to let her try climbing.

Jeannie didn't laugh when Kit referred to it as a "crash course," but she tried to remain as good-humored as possible. In any case, Pinnacles was a beautiful place. That helped soothe her. They were surrounded by jagged peaks of multicolored sandstone above patchwork carpets of spring flowers.

What Jeannie longed to do was lie on a patch of that carpet with Kit's arm behind her as she looked up at clouds blowing across the sky. What she did instead was allow herself to be roped between Kit and Dmitri as they prepared to climb a route known as Salathe's Sliver. There they demonstrated a procedure called belaying. Jeannie was between the boys, with a rope wrapped around her waist. She had to work, gripping the rock with her hands and feet, but she was protected by the rope that Kit had secured from above her.

As Kit gave instructions, she let herself fall to the end of the rope. The total distance of her fall was only three feet, yet it made her heart bump in her throat. After a minute, though, she realized that she was being held tightly by the harness. She was both free to climb and safe as she leaned back from the rock, searching for handholds and footholds. This was different from climbing without ropes. For the first time, she had some notion of how climbing made Kit feel. The simultaneous sensation of freedom and safety was very heady.

She would have liked to tell this to Kit, yet when she looked up to where he crouched on a ledge above her, his eyes had a strange, faraway look. He wasn't teaching a beginner at Pinnacles; he was already on his way up Half Dome. Occasionally, he leaned down and gave her advice, but for long stretches of time he seemed self-absorbed, remote.

Dmitri stayed with her. He soloed—climbed without the protection of the rope—alongside her so that with a word or gesture he could supply the details she needed to learn. He didn't use any frightening climbing jargon, either—just clear, patient words.

Kit tuned back in when it was time for her to learn how to rappel. With the belay rope secured above her head, she practiced bracing her feet against the rock and using the rope to lower herself back to the ground. Only after Kit was satisfied that she had learned this skill did he agree that she was ready to climb Flatiron.

Flatiron, the boys told her, was considered the most interesting of the one-pitch climbs. It was about one hundred and ten feet from the base to the summit. They had to go up a rock face, negotiate an overhang, and use a bolt ladder. On top was a spot where they could have lunch before using the ropes to rappel down. Jeannie was hesitant, worrying that maybe she was being stretched too far too fast, yet she did not protest. Both Dmitri and Kit assured her that she could climb it.

"I'll lead," Kit said. "Then, when it's your turn, take it easy. And don't worry. You can't fall, because you'll be on belay."

Jeannie was hot and light-headed by this time. The practice had been strenuous. Although she was tired, she felt good. As she looked up at Flatiron, her hesitation vanished. Suddenly, nothing seemed really frightening or dangerous. She was ready.

Dmitri belayed Kit as he started up, trailing the rope that was attached to Jeannie's harness. Occasionally Kit paused to clip the rope into fixed pitons. Jeannie watched him anxiously. After he had completed his first series of maneuvers, she realized how much his skills had improved. Since his surgery, he had become as graceful a climber as Dmitri. The ankle brace was visible, but the leg seemed to be strong.

Jeannie wished that her uncle were here to see this. Then he could understand that Kit was able to climb. Watching, she thought that Kit was at least as good as Dmitri now. Maybe even better.

Soon Kit disappeared around a rock ledge. All she saw now was the rope. She heard him, however. The sound of his feet on gritty sandstone, the labored breathing. At last, his voice reached her. "I made it. I'm up. But don't do anything yet."

He was over the pitch, up the ladder, and on top of Flatiron. Jeannie heard the click of a carabiner being attached to a piton and a slapping noise as he coiled up the excess rope. He pulled the rope up until it pulled on her, and, finally, he called down to her. "I have you on belay. Come on ahead."

While she was still close to the ground, she felt competent. She received advice both from Kit, who could not see her, and from Dmitri, who could. As she climbed higher, however, she started to shake in a now-familiar way. Not even the security provided by the rope kept her fear from returning.

When Kit's words came to her from above, his voice had a strange, remote quality. He sounded like the Yeti he had once described for her—untamed, untouchable. A creature of the mountains. Dmitri, by contrast, sounded like an athletic boy who was a senior at Jackson High. He seemed solid and real. Jeannie was glad to have him giving her advice.

Dmitri had solo–climbed up a ways so he could help supervise her holds. Flatiron, as Kit had told her, was a climb he had seen nine-year-olds do with their parents. At the time, that had been a reassuring statement, but it was not convincing while she wondered whether the tiny outcropping under her left boot was going to hold.

What she was doing seemed dangerous. She was worried. She was about to attempt the difficult moves necessary to lift herself around the overhang, and Kit was again calling down to her. "You'll be all right. There are buckets everywhere—for your feet and your hands. Don't freeze—just keep moving. Are you all right? Are you?"

Before she could answer, something happened. She heard unexpected noises—the click of metal, followed by a skidding sound and a clatter of pebbles from the summit. She froze.

"Kit!" Dmitri called out. "Kit! Are you all right?"

At first the only sound was another metallic click. Then Kit spoke in a remote, begrudging tone. "I'm fine."

"What happened?" Dmitri asked. "Were you clipped in? Did you have her on belay?"

Even before Kit gave his answer, Jeannie knew what he was going to say. No, she hadn't been on belay. No, Kit hadn't been clipped in. Her sense of well-being deserted her entirely. He wasn't supposed to be moving when she was climbing. He was supposed to be providing safety for her. If Kit had really slipped, they would have both fallen.

Kit's voice was thin, apologetic. "I was moving to a different spot. Wanted to see her come around the overhang. Help her on the ladder."

Jeannie had a lot of things she wanted to say, but she didn't have the strength to speak. She no longer cared about a picnic lunch on top of Flatiron. She wasn't interested in lying in the wild flowers with Kit. She was angry and afraid. She wanted to yell at him. She wanted to go home. And she did not think she ever wanted to be with Kit or watch him climb again.

After that, she relied exclusively on Dmitri for help. She climbed around the overhang and up the bolt ladder to the summit. Lunch was silent and tense. Only when she rappelled down off the rock did she have a momentary sense of relief and accomplishment. Then it vanished. Excusing herself, she clomped off toward the women's rest room, leaving the two boys to gather up the gear.

She took a long time washing her face, rearranging the pigtails she had worn for the occasion. She did not feel angry any more. She felt numb, unresponsive. By the time she made her way back to the car, the two boys were packed up and ready to go. She slid in next to Kit, sipped slowly at the warm Coke he opened for her, but she sat there staring out the window because she didn't have anything to say. Neither did he.

Two hours later, after Dmitri had been dropped at his house, Kit finally broke the silence. "I feel like a bear that's run into a beehive."

Jeannie frowned. "And I feel like a cub who trusted the bear and got stung."

"I'm sorry. Sorry for me and for you. Because you'll always think of me as crippled in one way or another. Because I let you down today, and knowing me, I'll do it again sometime."

She took a long time to think about what he had said. Then, pulling aimlessly at one pigtail, she answered. "What do you want from me, Kit? What?"

His eyes never left the road. "I want the same thing you want—someone I can count on."

Jeannie sighed helplessly. "You can count on me."

"Can I?" he asked. "It doesn't make me feel terrific to take my girl climbing and find she spends all her time listening to my best friend. Maybe I should move in on Lisabeth and see how that makes you feel."

Jeannie did not protest, not even feebly. When Kit was in this kind of mood, there was no reasoning with him. He was distraught because he'd put the two of them in danger by unclipping a carabiner. Now he was trying to shift guilt from himself to her. She did not like that. Nor was she sure she liked him referring to her as "his girl."

"Dmitri was just closer to me while you were out of sight," she said at last. "I think . . . I think we're back to Dr. Goldberger's old theory about wings and roots."

"What does that have to do with anything?"

"You," she continued, "are trying to get me to grow wings. Take risks. Write freer poems. Really try dancing."

"Am I wrong?" he asked.

"No. Except, as always, you try to push me too hard—and you do the same thing with yourself."

"So? Maybe I like it that way."

"So," she repeated, "Maybe *I* don't. You wing away with your writing, climbing, Birdmen, magic, photography, jazz, but you never stop to put down roots. I don't influence you as much as you influence me. If I did . . . you would not have unclipped me. You would have done the safe thing instead of the risky one."

Kit didn't answer. They rode in silence for a long while. Jeannie didn't look over at Kit, so she did not know how he was reacting to her words.

When Kit finally spoke, there was a husky tone to his voice. "You are right, Jeannie—and I am sorry. Truly sorry. But please don't give up on me. I need you."

Then he took his right hand from the wheel and groped for her left one. As he had done earlier that day, he pressed his nails into her palm.

"I need you," he repeated, putting his hand back on the wheel. "Forgive me. It's okay. Everything's going to be all right, isn't it?"

Jeannie bit down on her lower lip. The pressure of his hand, his apology had helped soothe her. But not quite enough.

20

As the music from *West Side Story* pounded in her head, Jeannie stretched and leaped across the floor of the dance studio. Her tights were black, but her new leotard was flame-colored.

"Jeannie," Flo called from her position near the phonograph, "head high. Loosen the neck, ease up on the shoulders. Yes, good. Now . . . . put more arch into that back. Try. Stretch!"

Although Jeannie tried, she knew that her back was as inflexible, her hamstrings as impossibly short as they had been when she danced with the Pacific Ballet. To dance, she would always have to move with a grace and energy meant to camouflage the handicaps she would never overcome.

Easing all words from her head, she let the sensuous rhythms of "Somewhere" and "I Feel Pretty" possess her. Like the ballerina in *The Red Shoes,* who danced because her life depended on it, Jeannie turned, reached, executed pliés and tour jetés. Jazz ballet had an excitement to it that she had never found in the still perfection of classical ballet.

Vaguely, she heard Flo's voice cautioning the other students to stop counting. Jeannie may have had an unyielding back, yet she never had to count the beat of the music. It was part of her, reverberating through her body as she danced.

Brightly colored images spun through her head as she and the others went through their routines. Images and more images. Climbing Flatiron. Working on one last edition of the *Banner* with Lisabeth. Kit smiling when he saw she had finally dared to publish a poem—a polished version of the one about fear.

As her feet and arms reached out, Jeannie saw Kit waving his acceptance letter from Harvard. She saw herself telling Martin she'd help with the summer program at Hanover. Kit running his fingers lightly through her hair. Graduation with her parents and Jill beaming proudly—with Kit as valedictorian talking about polio and Syl Goldberger, about every limit being a new beginning.

In blurry colors and textures, she saw the Senior Prom with Kit playing drums as she danced with a dozen boys whose names she hardly knew. Her meeting with Dr. Goldberger. Her conference with Flo. And Kit. Always Kit. Kit assembling his summer climbing gear piece by piece. Herself telling Martin she wanted to make some changes. And dancing, dancing . . .

With these images surrounding her, Jeannie realized that one of the reasons she could not shake Kit from her mind was that he was there, standing in one corner of the studio. He was watching intently.

He had come early, she knew, precisely because he wanted to see her dancing. Well, he was welcome. He could stare all he wanted, she decided, extending her whole body to match the strains of "Tonight." But then, too soon, the hour was over. Exuding fine beads of sweat, she gave Flo a quick wave and ran to join Kit.

"I'm late. And I stink. I'll shower in the nurses' quarters. But we do have to hurry. I'm sorry. Really sorry."

Her words came out in a jumble. She did not want to rush, yet her schedule was tight because she was dancing each morning before she began her day at the hospital. In order to say goodbye to her, Kit had volunteered to drive her from one place to the other.

Kit didn't seem to care that she hadn't showered. He had something else on his mind. "I think you made a mistake not to devote all summer to dancing."

Although Jeannie smiled up at him, she did not answer. She thought she had made the right decision.

"When you dance," Kit continued, "and I've just seen you once before, you look like I feel when I climb. But I've told you that, haven't I? So—why is it—why is it that you can't understand why I climb?"

That subject was, as always, dangerous territory. She had answers for him, but she held them back. She was determined that today's goodbye would not include one of their wild, shouting arguments.

Still, her tongue got the best of her. "When you are able to understand why I am back at the hospital, maybe I will be able to understand why you must climb mountains, must climb Half Dome."

"But I'm not doing Half Dome. Too hard. I'm not good enough. We've decided to do Royal Arches. It's a super climb, Jeannie, to a place with a spring at the top. A spot called the Jungle. And it's a climb I can do without pushing too hard."

Jeannie did not reply as Kit took her arm. Only his slightly uneven gait indicated that he had had polio, or suggested that climbing for him might be more difficult than for others.

With his usual persistence, Kit brought up Hanover again. "That place is too safe for you. It's something you've done before. You're there for your uncle—not for yourself. It's territory you've covered. All the climbing I'm doing this summer will be new territory."

"Kit . . . oh, Kit, please," Jeannie urged as they got

into his family's car. "Let's not start in, please. I *am* going to be trying something new."

"What?"

"Dance therapy with some of Syl's patients."

"You never told me that."

"You never asked."

"But, Jeannie, you're still inside that hospital and—"

"Cut it out," she said, interrupting. "You're going away and I want it to be good."

Kit stopped badgering her immediately. He, too, seemed to want them to part on good terms. When they were sitting in the car outside Hanover, the subjects of hospitals and climbing were left untouched. Instead, they sat for a few minutes just looking at one another.

Jeannie tried to decide what the two of them were to one another now. Certainly she was no longer "his girl," and he was no longer a boyfriend. Though they went through the last two months of school without any visible breakup, since Flatiron things had not been the same. They had been together, yet they had been apart, too. Although it made Jeannie feel wistful at times, it also made her feel freer, less responsible for Kit's welfare.

"You look like a jelly bean," Kit said companionably. "What's happened to the licorice stick?"

Laughing, Jeannie shrugged. "Got tired of looking like I was in mourning. Decided that wearing black was not improving my poetry."

"I liked the licorice look. Thought it made you different, distinguished, Jeannie with the light-brown hair."

Her fingers and toes prickled as they always did when he called her that. She blew him a kiss. Then she laughed again. "I know that. But, let's face it, I think I *like* being a bright piece of candy. So—take it or leave it."

Kit's face grew serious. "I think I am about to leave it. That's why I'm here, remember?"

"I remember," Jeannie answered quietly.

Absentmindedly, Kit tugged at a lock of her hair. "I remember, too—a lot of things, good and bad. Bad and good. Are we still friends?"

"Of course!" Jeannie insisted as she reached down into her green bag and pulled out a small leather-bound notebook. It was the same one she had tried to give him a year and half before. "I have a present for you . . . to take climbing . . ."

Kit reached for the notebook. "With your poems in it?"

"One of them. But the rest is for you. For you to use for your own writing."

"But I'm not doing any writing," Kit protested darkly. "And I thought we'd given up trying to influence one another."

"Yes, I guess. But . . . no—never. Didn't I just hear you complaining for the hundredth time that I'm back at the hospital? And didn't you just say you liked me better in black?"

It was Kit's turn to laugh. Instead of answering her questions, however, he opened the notebook and looked at the poem inscribed on the first page. Using the sensitive, measured cadence of his valedictorian voice, he read it aloud.

Wings and Roots

"Every limit . . ."

He has wings
strong and sure
so he can soar with ease,
take risks,
feel the limits of the sky.

183

"Every limit is ..."
She has roots
deep and probing
so she can grow tall,
   hold fast,
     taste the goodness of the earth.

"Every limit is a beginning ..."

Hearing the mingled tunes
of one another's songs,
he has learned
    of roots
as she has learned
     of wings.

Now strong, sure, deep,
probing, feeling, tasting—
   taking risks, yet holding fast,
may they both soar and grow.

"Every limit is a beginning as well as an ending."

       Jeanne-Marie West

When Kit finished reading, he didn't make any comment. Closing the notebook, he placed it on the seat between them, with his fingertips lightly touching hers. She didn't move her hand. She wanted to hear what he thought of the poem, but at the same time she did not want him to say a word. She was happy. She was sad. She was not going to cry. Still, her head felt full of tears. Full of words, too. Always more words.

All of a sudden, she wanted to get out of the car and up the steps. "I've got to go. I'm late. My head's swimming ..."

"Jeannie," Kit said, pressing his nails into her palm, "you are always swimming. You are . . . like a beautiful rainbow trout, moving gracefully downstream . . ."

She squeezed his hand. "And you," she replied, taking up his simile and extending it, "are like a determined salmon thrashing his way upstream against all odds."

Kit's eyes were bright as he smiled. He pulled his hand away from hers. "Not bad. Now open that door. Move. Go on, before we both cry!"

Needing no further encouragement, Jeannie jumped out. Before she had a chance to slam the door, Kit's voice came barking from behind her. "Hey, you—nurse, pick up my pencil. I'm a polio!"

Jeannie leaned on the door and looked back at Kit. "Get lost!" she said. "As I'm a dancer, a hospital aide . . . a poet—you're a drummer, a climber, a writer. But you are not a polio, Kit. Now, good luck on the Arches—and goodbye!"

Then she flipped the door shut and ran, letting the warm, stinging tears flow freely from her eyes.

*   *   *

what do you want from me, you asked, and i with no understanding said, i want someone i can count on. now it is late and i am resting several thousand feet above a great valley. as i gaze out at the vast and beautiful vistas, i see that between us there is something real and unchanging, not dependent upon the whims of chance or romance. for all time

1 8 5

we are, as are these mountains, even when we are miles or worlds apart. i know now that i can count on you, for we may differ but what we have will change yet still endure.

YETI

I did it, Jeannie! With help from Dmitri, I am on top of Royal Arches, in the Jungle by the spring. I have come a long, long way. And I am crying to think you cannot be here, my dear friend.

Your friend,
Christopher Hayden